The
House
Filler

THE CHINA CHINA TRILOGY

Book I

The House Filler

1918–1966

The House Filler

Tong Ge

RONSDALE PRESS

THE HOUSE FILLER
Copyright © 2023 Tong Ge

RONSDALE PRESS
125A — 1030 Denman Street, Vancouver, B.C. Canada V6G 2M6
www.ronsdalepress.com

Typesetting: Julie Cochrane
Cover Design: David Lester

Ronsdale Press wishes to thank the following for their support of its publishing program: the Canada Council for the Arts, the Government of Canada, the British Columbia Arts Council, and the Province of British Columbia through the British Columbia Book Publishing Tax Credit program.

Library and Archives Canada Cataloguing in Publication

Title: The house filler : a novel / Tong Ge.
Names: Ge, Tong, author.
Identifiers: Canadiana (print) 20230485588 | Canadiana (ebook) 2023048560X | ISBN 9781553806981 (softcover) | ISBN 9781553806998 (EPUB) | ISBN 9781553807001 (PDF)
Classification: LCC PS8613.E225 H68 2023 | DDC C813/.6—dc23

At Ronsdale Press we are committed to protecting the environment. To this end, we are working with Canopy and printers to phase out our use of paper produced from ancient forests. This book is one step towards that goal.

Printed in Canada

To my grandmother

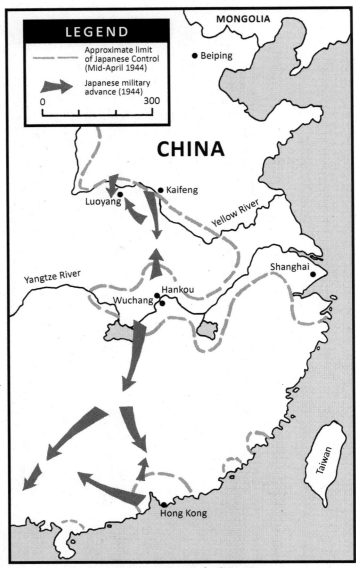

Credit: U.S. Army Center of Military History

LIST OF CHARACTERS

Golden Phoenix — Hu Jinfeng (胡金凤)
Rui (睿)
Yu (裕)
Li Haichun (李海春)
Li Zhong (李忠)
Li Xiao (李孝)
Li Wen (李文)
Li Wu (李武)
Daisy — Li Xiuju (李秀菊)
Orchid — Li Xiulan (李秀兰)
Qi (奇)
Primrose (樱子)
Li Xicai (李喜财)
Mrs. Lin (林太)
Snowflake — Xuehua (雪花)
Chang Cheng (长城)
Big Ox — Daniu (大牛)
Star (星星)
Moon (月月)
Hui (慧)
Ming (明)
Tong Shu (童舒)
Tong Yao — Yaoyao (童谣 — 谣谣)

Spring Review
DU FU[1]

On war-torn land rivers flow, mountains stand.
In vernal town grass and weeds are overgrown.
Grieved over the years, flowers make us shed tears.
Hating to part, hearing birds breaks our heart.
For three months, beacon fires have burned,
Letters from home are worth their weight in gold.
I cannot bear to scratch my grizzling hair;
it's grown too thin to hold a light hairpin.

（春望
国破山河在， 城春草木深。 感时花溅泪， 恨别鸟惊心。
烽火連三月， 家书抵万金。白头搔更短，渾欲不胜簪。）

---

[1] Du Fu (712–770) was one of the most outstanding poets in the Tang
dynasty. The poem is translated by Xu Yuanchong and modified by
Tong Ge.

Peace Time

KAIFENG CITY,
HENAN PROVINCE

1918–1937

Chapter 1

I met the man I grew to love and the man I came to hate on the same day.

I had waited for that day for ten long years and lost hope of getting married. When most girls are married off at age sixteen, a twenty-six-year-old unmarried woman is considered an old maid. A fresh lad was out of my reach. The villagers believed my best chance was to marry a widower and become a *tianfang*—a house filler.

Then, out of nowhere, Father received a marriage proposal through the shop owner in Kaifeng who acted as a middleman for my opera costume-making business. However, the widower was twenty years my senior.

"Too old for you. I turned him down," Father told me that night.

Within days, Father received a second marriage proposal. This man, also a widower, was only ten years my senior. Father met him in the middleman's shop in Kaifeng. When Father came home, he announced, "Jinfeng, it's decided. At least he is mature, not bad-looking and has his own business. I can't let this one pass."

"Did he ask . . . ?"

"No, he didn't ask about your feet." Father waved his tobacco pipe dismissively.

On the day before my wedding, Father sat in our court-yard after supper. Outside, the sun turned from bright white to golden, then to the colour of fire persimmon. The typical heat wave in summer had subsided to a comfortable warm breeze. While he was cooling off with the big plantain fan, I was in the kitchen boiling water for a bath. Throwing dry corn stalks and twigs into the belly of the stove, I pushed and pulled the handle of the wind chamber. Sweat trickled down my forehead to my cheeks and chin, then dropped onto the ground, evaporating within seconds, leaving no trace behind.

Since I was motherless, the Hu clan had sent a woman to our house and told me what would happen on my wedding night.

"You saw how animals mate, it's just like that," she said.

Like animals? My face burned like a hot iron. I lowered my head.

"Take a bath today, for you may not have the time tomorrow. Make sure to wash your feet well, and remember, you must always obey your husband." With those words, the woman left.

Why especially feet? Was she implying my feet were stinky? I was a bit offended. Even with the scarce water supply, I made sure to wash my feet every day. Besides, the foot bathwater was always used to water the flowers in the yard so nothing was wasted. Women's bound feet were private in those days. The only people who had seen and touched mine were my father and the two witches who bound them. Since I was too young, he took on the daily routine of unwrapping, washing and rewrapping my feet. It was not a man's job. With his big hands, he did it clumsily at first, then gradually got better. When I was seven, I learned to do it myself.

I closed my bedroom door, lit one single candle, and stepped into the small wooden bath basin. In the flickering shadows of the candlelight, my deformed feet looked like two pointed horse hooves. After walking for so many years on my four-*cun*[2] silver water lily feet—one cun too large to be a perfect bride—I no longer felt the initial sharp pain, only the ache after a long day. I scraped my skin slowly and methodically, including the deep grooves between my heels and insteps, and wondered how women's distorted feet were considered attractive. Most Chinese men had a foot fetish for the three-cun "golden water lilies." Playing with such feet gave them the utmost pleasure. All this was because of a damn emperor in the Song dynasty nine centuries ago who liked tiny-footed women.

After China became a republic in 1912, our founding father, Sun Zhongshan,[3] formally abolished foot-binding. But it seemed that only some big city folks welcomed the change. I learned this from my brother Rui's letter. As the eldest son in our family, Father sent him to Shanghai at age sixteen. He started as an accounting clerk in a

---

[2] 1 *cun* = 1.31 inch

[3] Sun Zhongshan, (1866–1925) also known as Sun Yat-sen or Sun Wen, was a Chinese statesman, physician and political philosopher. He served as the first provisional president of the Republic of China and was the first leader of the Nationalist Party of China. He is widely regarded as the "Father of the Nation" in the Republic of China and the "Forerunner of the Revolution" in the People's Republic of China for his instrumental role in the overthrow of the Qing dynasty during the Xinhai Revolution of 1911–1912.

shipping company, climbed all the way up to chief accountant, married and had a daughter who escaped the torture of foot-binding.

But in Henan province, having three-cun golden water lilies was still seen as a woman's most desirable feature. How could my husband-to-be have forgotten to ask about my feet? When he discovered my four-cun feet on our wedding night, what would happen? Would he be angry and regretful? Or even divorce me?

A whiff of tobacco smoke drifted from Father's pipe into the room, mixing with the smell of the mud walls, the dirt floor, the old furniture and the new clothes. The room was hot and stuffy. Our three hens and ten chicks, purchased in the spring, were settling down on the roost in the courtyard, whispering their little secrets. The moonlight grew brighter, casting swaying tree shadows onto my paper-covered latticed window. A crow's caw startled the night. *A bad omen.* Hopefully, I'd see magpies the next day; they were always a good omen.

"Go to bed early. You'll have a long day tomorrow," Father shouted from the yard. I heard him knock off the ash from his smoking pipe and saunter into his room, then shut the door.

I had a hard time falling asleep. A mosquito had gotten into my mosquito net, but I couldn't find it. It drove me mad. Finally, I took the net off the ceiling, scrunched it with the mosquito into a ball and threw it in the corner of the bed. The mice were also particularly noisy, running

---

4 Mice getting married is a common theme in Chinese fantasies and folk tales.

on the ceiling as if they were fighting or having a wedding procession.[4]

Would my husband be nice to me? What did he look like? What kind of people were my in-laws? All mothers-in-law were mean. As the Chinese saying goes, a daughter-in-law is made by beating just as dough is made by kneading. I only hoped I wouldn't be kneaded too hard.

When I finally drifted off, I dreamed of my wedding night. My husband, upon seeing my feet, cried out, fell off the bed and became a big scary mouse. I woke up in a fright and could not fall back to sleep.

Chapter 2

When the rooster crowed for the third time, I dragged myself up and began to make breakfast: millet congee, re-steamed buns, pickled cucumbers and white radish. I gulped down a bowl of congee and a bun, as I knew I wouldn't have time for lunch.

The women from the Hu clan arrived. They removed the fine hairs on my face with thread, combed my hair and perfumed it with osmanthus oil, and coiffed my long braid into a bun behind my skull, securing it with a silver hairpin—the only item I'd inherited from my mother. Long braids were for maidens; buns were for married women. Not long ago, Chinese men also wore long braids. When the revolution came, the Qing dynasty was no more, and as citizens of the new republic, Chinese men were asked to cut off their braids. But it was hard. For many of them, losing their braid was losing their dignity. Other men kept their braids out of loyalty to the old Imperial family or fear of Qing's army's return. One day, my father went to Kaifeng and bumped into a group of students who were hunting down men with braids. Father was pinned against a wall, while they cut off his braid. Afterwards, he covered his head with a dog-skin trapper hat for months, ashamed to let anyone see his new hairstyle. Fortunately, it was winter.

Thinking of this, I chuckled involuntarily.

"You're supposed to cry your eyes out on your wedding day." An auntie gave me a light shove. Normally, brides cried when they were about to leave their beloved parents behind. A laughing bride could be seen as heartless and improper. But those girls were sixteen and seventeen. To a twenty-six-year-old, getting married was a huge relief. Still, I knew I needed to be reserved and serious.

While the women helped me with makeup, my thoughts drifted to my mother, who died giving birth to me. I had learned from my brothers that my mother died before having a chance to feed me even once. During the initial days, the new mothers in the village took turns feeding me. Later, Father bought a goat to feed me its milk. When I was a bit older, Father made millet gruel and wheat flour congee for me, and even added smashed egg yolk from time to time. He was the one who changed my diapers, bathed me and taught me to walk and talk. After my brothers left home, I was the only child at my father's side. Now, in less than twelve *shichen*—twenty-four hours in Western time—I would depart the only house I knew and leave my father forever.

"Don't cry now! You'll mess up your makeup," scolded a woman helping me. I quickly dabbed away my tears and looked at myself in the mirror, taking in the duck egg-shaped face and double eyelids, typical beauty elements in Chinese culture. With drawn eyebrows and powdered cheeks, I could almost be considered pretty if my skin colour were lighter. Chinese believe that one fair skin covers up one hundred uglinesses. However, in comparison to the size of my feet, my dark skin was a minor flaw. How I hoped that my future husband could overlook both. To compensate, I would try my best to use my strong points—my needlework, my good heart and my diligence.

On my bed, my wedding clothes were laid out: a Chinese-style blouse with an opening on the side and a pair of pants, both made of red silk. As a seamstress, I added my special touch by embroidering lacework in golden thread on the high collar, sleeve and trouser cuffs. I also made my own wedding shoes with a smiling brocade golden phoenix embroidered on the vamp. The design was my favourite because my first name—Jinfeng—means golden phoenix.

The women chirped like sparrows.

"How lucky you are, finding a man in Kaifeng."

"Look at those wedding clothes. You made—"

"We country bumpkins can't ask for more."

"Once you're gone, where do we get embroidery patterns?"

"I heard he is a tile flipper, has a big house—"

"Aiya! You stepped on me!"

"As long as he lives with his parents, the house is not—"

"If you want to earn his family's respect, have a baby boy."

"If not, he may get himself a second wife."

My brand new white muslin foot-bandages were neatly wrapped around my feet. I had a red scarf ready to cover my face when arriving at my husband's house. No one there was supposed to see my face until the groom took the scarf veil off. It would be the first time we saw each other.

The departure time came. Tradition required me to go

there alone. As I stepped outside my room, I saw that the entire village had come to see me off. Weddings and funerals were always a village affair. Everyone would show up unless the family had enemies. Father had no enemy, and I sure hoped I wouldn't end up with one either.

A hen clucked proudly; she must have just laid an egg. The Chinese date trees were blossoming with little yellow-greenish flowers. In just a few months, the dates would be ready for harvesting. Father's potted flowers also bloomed vigorously in the yard. Once I left, he would have to rely on selling those potted flowers—not much of an income. Father had sold the few mu^5 of land we once had to pay for my brothers' schooling shortly after my mother passed away. The room against the east wall looked shabby. It was once my brothers' classroom. After Rui left home, my other brother, Yu, didn't want to study anymore, so Father let go of the tutor and turned it into a storage room.

Firecrackers ignited noisily. Kids covered their ears with their hands. Red and white confetti littered the ground. Dogs barked and babies cried. The acrid gunpowder smell overtook the sweet scent of the flowers in the yard.

The women helped me to put on the veil so that no stranger could see my face as I stepped out of our courtyard. I was helped into the bright red palanquin carried by eight men, and we took off. An eight-carrier palanquin was typical for a maiden becoming a first wife but even though I was a house filler, the groom had agreed to do this for me. The palanquin creaked as if singing a happy tune. A group of musicians playing trumpets led the

---

[5] 1 *mu* = 0.16 acre

procession, followed by eight more men carrying four trunks of my dowry. In other provinces, a man had to pay a bride price to get married. Not in Henan. Here, the bride needed a dowry to be married off. The larger the dowry she brought with her, the more respect she would get in her husband's house. I had seen ten trunks of dowry from rich brides and none from poor ones. According to the old folks in the village, during a famine, a girl being sold for a sack of grain was not uncommon. In many cases, the girls ended up in whorehouses.

Tradition required me to cover my face even inside the palanquin, but the moment the palanquin's front curtain was lowered, I took the veil off. As the noise behind us trailed off, I opened the side curtain a crack and peeked back. Father stood on a raised well platform at the edge of the village, one hand shading his eyes, looking in my direction. At age sixty, his hair had turned white. Once I left home, he would have to fetch water from the well, cook and clean all by himself. He could have kept his sons at home, as most villagers did. But he wanted them to have a better life, so he sent Rui to Shanghai. As for Yu, Father couldn't make him study or work, so he sent him to live with Rui, hoping big brother could lead little brother to the right path.

The musicians had stopped playing their instruments. No need to make a show on an empty country road. I peered out from the crack of the curtain. It was June. The sun baked the earth. The wheat field had turned yellow, the kernels heavy and the heads bent low. The smell of harvest was in the air. Sweat dampened my clothes and I felt parched and suffocated, just like the last time I was stuffed into a palanquin when I was nineteen.

Chapter 3

Seamstress Liu had persuaded my father to enter me into the annual bound-feet contest in the famous Xiangguo Temple, a temple built over a thousand years ago in Kaifeng.

"A girl is never yours. She belongs to another family. You knew this the moment she was born. You don't want an old maid on your hand, do you?" Seamstress Liu clucked like an old hen.

At age twelve, Father sent me to her to learn the trade. By age sixteen, I was able to make costumes for opera singers. I earned such a reputation that they would send their orders to me through a middleman in Kaifeng, and Father was my delivery man. Since I had become the family breadwinner, Father seemed to have forgotten about arranging for my marriage.

I overheard their conversation in our courtyard.

"With her feet, she'll never win the contest," Father said.

"Perhaps you don't know how it works. Most girls participating in the contest have no hope of winning. But they may get marriage proposals from the audience."

Father finally agreed.

On *xia zhi*, the first day of summer, I was stuffed into

a palanquin with the curtains drawn, revealing only my bound feet. I wore a light cyan, high-collared silk shirt and a pair of black silk pants. My long hair was perfumed with osmanthus oil and neatly braided into a plait reaching my waist.

One winner would be chosen, judged by the size of her feet and the needlework on her shoes, which must be made by the contestant herself. On each red satin vamp, I had embroidered a golden phoenix. She flew upward, her wings outstretched, covering the vamp. To make this phoenix special, instead of a beady eye, I made her eye resemble a thin, waxing crescent moon, as if she were smiling. Even though I knew I wouldn't win, I hoped someone would be attracted by my exquisite needlework and present a marriage proposal to my father.

Twenty palanquins were assembled in the middle of the open space of the temple, mine being the twentieth. We sat in the palanquins for hours. Despite the silk garments—the coolest material—it was difficult to breathe in the enclosed space. I cracked the curtain and peeked out. Hundreds of people—men, women, children—were gathered. Firecrackers exploded, signalling the start of the contest. I closed the curtain and listened to the comments on our feet and shoes.

"Look at number twenty! What beautiful shoes," said a woman's voice.

A man's voice replied, "But look at her feet. They are not three-cun water lilies. They are boats."

I bit my lip.

"Why do you care about her feet?" said the woman's voice. "Don't tell me you are here to find a concubine."

"Nonsense. I'm thinking of our son."

"In that case, her feet are a bit too large. Our son deserves the best. What a pity! She probably will end up with a common labourer."

If their son was of marriageable age, the man must be old. If my feet were like boats, his must be like ocean liners. Of course, men needn't be concerned about the size of their feet. All they needed to worry about was money and success. The more money a man had, the more wives he could get. With the revolution, what did a man lose? Only the braid on the back of his head. Women must yield to men's desire, even to the point of deforming their feet.

I didn't receive any marriage proposals, even though many admired my needlework. Father and I never again talked about the contest or my getting married.

A man's voice brought me back to the present, "Let's get some rest."

They lowered my palanquin to the ground, but I was not allowed to step out to face the male strangers. From the shade, I knew we were under a big tree. I heard them chat and drink water, and I smelled tobacco and the sour smell of sweat and dust, together with the fresh smell of grass.

A man told a dirty joke. Others laughed presumptuously. Another man started to sing at the top of his lungs from the opera *Mu Guiying in Command*:

Outside the gate, three cannon shots echoed like
    thunder,
I, the general who guarded her country, walks out
    from the Tianbo mansion.
With a golden crown on my head and my hair
    neatly arranged,

I put on the iron armour I once wore in the past.
The commanding flag flutters like a cloud,
Emblazoned with the name *Huntian Marquis Mu
    Guiying*.
The character Mu, as big as a *dou*,[6] shakes heaven
    and earth.
Who would have thought that at age fifty-three,
    I would once again lead the military?

(辕门外三声炮如同雷震，天波府里走出来我保国臣。头戴金冠
压双鬓，当年的铁甲我又披上身。
帅字旗，飘如云，斗大的穆字震乾坤。上写着浑天侯穆氏桂英，
谁料想我五十三岁又管三军。)

The man was imitating a soprano, and he did a pretty
good job. How I loved the story! Set in the Song dynasty, *Mu Guiying in Command* was a classic and often per-
formed by different opera companies—I had even made
costumes for them! According to the legend, the military
family of Yang led their armies to fight off the invading
Liao from the north and saved the country. Mu Guiying,
a trained warrior who married into the Yang family, was
a key figure in this fight. Over the years, the seven sons
and two grandsons of the family sacrificed their lives for
their country. Twenty years later, when Liao invaded Song
again, Mu Guiyang, just like her grandmother-in-law, led
the army and defeated the enemy.

Kaifeng—the place we were heading to—had been
the capital during the Song dynasty. I was excited at the

---

[6] 1 *dou* = 10 litres

thought of living there from this day on. My palanquin was lifted, and we were on our way again.

Women raised as martial artists or warriors didn't have their feet bound. I wished I was a warrior with natural feet and could ride horses and shoot arrows. But I was not a warrior, nor could I escape the destiny of most women—to be a good daughter-in-law, a good wife and, one day, a good mother. A woman's worth was measured by three things: the size of her feet, the quality of her needlework and her cooking skills. I had lost on the first one but hoped to gain some points on my needlework. As for my cooking skills, my in-laws would be the judges.

The palanquin came to a halt at the city gate and was lowered to the ground for a brief rest. Then the musicians enthusiastically began to trumpet, and we set off again. My wedding outfit was soaked with sweat, and my throat was on fire with thirst. I heard kids alongside my palanquin shouting, "Look at the bride," even though they couldn't see a thing. The street grew noisier—footsteps shuffled, peddlers called out, horses clattered on the paved street and donkeys brayed. There were also sounds unique to a big city: ringing bicycles and honking motorcars. A strong smell of food drifted in. We must have passed a restaurant, then a fruit stand, then horse manure. I was glad I was in an eight-carrier palanquin with a grand public wedding procession—the highest honour for a bride—not like a concubine sneaking into her husband's house through a side door in a two-carrier palanquin.

When we stopped again and the palanquin was lowered to the ground, someone announced our arrival. I draped the scarf over my head in a hurry. The front curtain was lifted, and two women helped me to step out. Since I could only see the tips of my feet, they guided me to step over a doorsill and down a brick path. I counted thirty steps to the second doorsill. It meant the first courtyard was quite big. After I crossed the second threshold, I counted another twenty-four steps; then we stopped. The two women who held my arms told me the brazier was right in front of me. It was to block any ghosts and demons that may have followed the bride and to burn away any bad luck that she might have brought with her. With the support of the two women, I crossed the brazier without incident. Next, I needed to stamp on the ceramic tiles laid out for me, to trample one's past and start a new life.

When I stepped on the tiles, my legs began to shake.

Memories of the agonizing days and sleepless nights that followed my foot-binding rushed back to me. Initially, I would unwrap the bandages at night and put my burning feet against the wall to soothe them. But freeing my feet made the foot-binding process impossible to complete, so the two aunties resorted to the ultimate foot-binding method. For a week, they held me down, wrapped shards of broken tile under the soles of my feet and forced me to walk on them. The sharp pieces soon sliced and rubbed off patches of skin. Blood stained my shoes and smudged the ground. With each bloody footprint, my dislocated toes were broken one by one. Only then did I realize the broken ceramic tile was used to break these bones.

All that suffering was for this day, but my legs were like noodles.

"Stamp harder," one woman urged.

"Come on," the other encouraged.

I heard murmurs from the onlookers. I steadied myself, said to the women, "Hold me tight," and jumped with both feet. The tiles shattered, and a searing pain shot through me from the bottom of my feet to the top of my head. If not for the two helpers, I would have collapsed and made a spectacle of myself.

After crossing the next doorsill, I was told we were in the guest hall.

I stood facing into the room, and someone handed me one end of a silk ribbon that was stretched to my left side. According to tradition, I knew the groom was holding the other end of the ribbon. "You are now facing your in-laws," the woman by my side whispered to me.

The wedding ceremony began. The noise around us quieted down. A man called out for us to *ketou* to Heaven and Earth. So I knelt and tapped my head to the ground. Then we ketoued to my in-laws. Then the bride and groom were called to bow to each other. After that, the same voice announced, "Li Haichun and Hu Jinfeng: you are husband and wife from this moment on."

According to the custom, the groom lifted my veil using a *cheng gan*—Chinese weight lever—because the word "cheng" shares the same pronunciation with the word "satisfied," implying that the groom is satisfied with the bride. I gave him a quick glance and lowered my gaze, as a proper woman should. But in that brief moment, our eyes met, and I saw kindness in his. He was a tall, hand-some man in a sparkly blue gown with two red silk sashes criss-crossed on his chest. In the middle was a big red silk flower—the standard decoration for a groom.

The wedding rules had been relaxed in recent years. In

the old days, a bride had to remain covered until the night of the wedding, and the only person who was allowed to see her face was the groom.

Looking up, I saw an old couple with silver hair sitting stiffly, facing us. They had to be my in-laws. From their straight faces, I couldn't read if I was welcome or not. Between them was a red wooden *ba xian zhuo*—a table for the eight immortals. Then, holding my elbow lightly, my husband guided me to a table on the side to sign our marriage certificate. I knew his name was Li Haichun but couldn't read it. I didn't even know how to write my own name. Times like this made me feel inadequate. My husband wrote his name beautifully with a brush pen. I, on the other hand, had to resort to a red fingerprint impression as my signature. *This is it*, I told myself. *I will spend the rest of my life with the man who stands beside me.*

Twenty temporary banquet tables were set up in both outer and inner courtyards, with ten stools around each table, so two hundred guests would show up—a typical wedding banquet for a well-off household. After the signing, my husband led me to our table directly facing the head table, where my in-laws sat. Other than "this way," "watch your step," and "here we are," he didn't say much. After all, we were there on display, not to get to know each other. Even so, he seemed to be attentive and mature. How I wished we would get along well and have a full house of children one day. The guests drifted in. Chicken, duck, fish, pork, vegetable dishes and noodles were served while guests drank the wine, partook of the feast and chatted noisily.

When the banquet was over, elderly guests began to leave. My in-laws also retired to their room. Younger guests remained. They were waiting for the *nao dong fang*—to play practical jokes on the newlyweds. Regardless of how rude or out of line the teasing went, the couple was not supposed to get upset or angry because people believed the more outrageous the jokes were, the more thriving the newlyweds' marriage life would be. The guests usually hid firecrackers just outside of the *new room*, the bedroom prepared for the newlyweds, and when they were about to make love, lit off the firecrackers to scare the daylights out of them. In some cases, the teasers even managed to hide inside the new room, under the bed, to witness the lovemaking. In one extreme case, a mountain village's nao dong fang turned into a nightmare. A group of young men tied up the groom in his room, then dragged the bride to a hillside and tied her to a tree. The villagers wanted to see how desperate the groom would be to rescue her. The next morning, people returned to the hillside tree only to find out that the bride had been eaten by wolves. The story was in the newspaper when I was a teen, and I didn't know if the group was punished by law or not.

Fortunately, our guests didn't do anything too wild, perhaps because both my husband and his friends were middle-aged. Mature people usually were not as crazy as young ones. I only needed to light cigarettes for male guests. As I lit them, they would blow out the flame, making me do it again and again. Even so, I was exhausted and felt lightheaded. I told myself, *hold on, just a little longer, don't shake, don't fall.* This was the most important date of my life; I could not make my husband and my in-laws lose face.

My husband accompanied me until someone called him

over. As I walked toward a table at the far end of the yard, a buck-toothed woman greeted me, "You're so lucky. On your wedding day, you already have a daughter-in-law."

I froze. "What?"

"This is your daughter-in-law." The woman turned to a plump, pock-faced woman sitting next to her.

Pock-face said to me, "My husband, Qi, is your stepson. He's over there." She chinned toward a man two tables away. Leaning against a chair, a tall, thin man who resembled my husband looked in our direction. His lopsided smile froze halfway, not quite reaching his eyes. The way he stood reminded me of a crooked tree. These two were not much younger than I was. How could this be? My husband had never told my father about his adult son. In fact, he told my father that his son was dead. If this woman was indeed my stepdaughter-in-law, I was one generation above her. Yet she didn't even bother to stand up.

My ears began to ring, and I no longer could hear words, only a buzz. My head was heavy and my feet light. I grabbed the edge of the table to steady myself.

"You don't look well. Let me take you to your seat." Pock-face held onto my arm and guided me back to my table. As she tried to push me onto my seat, I glanced down. To my horror, a handful of date tree thorns was piled on the seat.

As I looked around, trying to figure out who did this, the tables and faces swirled, and my vision blurred. I slipped to the ground like a fish, then blacked out.

Chapter 4

I woke to find a damp cloth pressed against my forehead. Faces hovered over me, and I heard people sigh with relief. Then, my husband scooped me up and carried me to our new room. After putting me in the bed, he asked me what happened. Holding back tears, I told him about the date tree thorns. He stared at me for a moment, seeming to decide if I was telling the truth.

"Have a rest. I need to go to see the guests off," he simply said, then left the room.

Where was the tenderness? Where was the care? Was he angry with me for ruining my own wedding and making him lose face? I lay in bed, trying to figure out who could have done such a wicked thing. Who hated me that much? I didn't know anybody here. How could I have made enemies? I had been prepared for this night since the winter morning my father came home with a box of sweet green bean cakes—my favourite.

I was six years old.

My brothers eyed the cake box like two hungry wolves. To my surprise, Father said, "These are for Golden Phoenix. The class is cancelled today. Finish your breakfast and I'll take you boys into the city."

"What about me?" I protested.

"You are to wait for the aunties from the Hu clan," Father said.

"I don't want aunties. I want to go with you." I almost burst into tears.

"Be a good girl. They are here to make you beautiful. By the way, you can eat as many cakes as you want," Father said, and they left.

All the cakes are for me? Whenever we had special treats, Father always divided them equally between us. I opened the box and found ten golden cakes, each imprinted with a lotus flower pattern. I picked up one flaky cake, the size of my palm, and carefully took a bite. It was dry but soon melted in my mouth. I finished the cake in no time flat, then took another one. When I finished the fifth, I felt sick to my stomach and had to stop.

Two familiar looking women walked in, one plump and one skinny. "Look at our pretty Golden Phoenix," the plump one said. "We'll make you even prettier."

"I'll boil some water," the skinny auntie said to the plump one, leaving the room for the kitchen. Outside, the snow had stopped, and the sun cast a bright glow through the windows. The plump auntie led me by the hand to our guest hall, sat down on a stool and placed me on her lap.

"Do you want beautiful feet?"

"Yes," I said shyly. Her hand was soft and warm. I had never been held by my mother and wanted to be held like this forever.

The skinny auntie came in with a wash basin filled with water. She placed the basin on the floor and put a bowl of crystal powder beside it.

"What's that?" I asked.

"Alum powder."

"What's it for?"

"To make your skin tight."

The skinny auntie took off my shoes, peeled off my socks and soaked my feet in the warm water. I looked at my feet. The skin was smooth and tight. Why did it need to be tighter?

After they dried my feet and clipped my toenails, one auntie held me while the other massaged my feet gently. I had never been pampered like this. *Maybe this is what mothers do for their children.* I was so happy, I wanted to cry.

A look passed between the two women, and the plump auntie's grip on my arms suddenly tightened. The skinny auntie grasped the second toe of my right foot between her thumb and index finger and bent it down—hard. When she let go, my toe went limp.

I howled and squirmed to get away. *What had I done wrong? Why had my father left me with these monsters?*

"It's dislocated," the skinny woman said to the plump one, ignoring my crying.

"Let me go, let me go!" In my struggle, I kicked over the wash basin, and water splashed everywhere.

"Be still. The more you fight it, the longer this takes. We have all gone through this. You are not the only one," the plump auntie whispered in my ears, her fingernails digging into my flesh. The skinny auntie bent my middle toe. The pain radiated to my head, and my body twisted like a snake.

When the skinny auntie bent my third toe, I threw up.

The green bean cakes were wasted. Pinching her nostrils with two fingers, the skinny auntie wiped the vomit from my clothes with a damp cloth, then gripped and bent the little toe with a pop. I passed out.

When I woke up, my right foot was wrapped tightly in white cloth, resembling a pointed horse hoof. They'd left my big toe alone. *Where are my other four toes?*

As if she could read my thoughts, the plump auntie said, "Your other toes are underneath your foot."

When she began to work on my left foot, I passed out again. Drifting in and out of consciousness, I didn't know how much time had passed. When I felt a cool, damp cloth wiping my face, I opened my eyes.

"Today's work is done. All your eight toes are only dislocated. If you don't want any more pain, do as you are told. First, you must walk. Your skin may tear but don't worry. The alum powder between your toes will prevent infection."

They helped me to put on a pair of tiny pink shoes embroidered with butterflies and gingerly put me on the floor. A thousand needles pierced my feet all at once. I cried out.

"Let's give her a break," the plump auntie said. "After all, she's not our daughter."

"If she were mine, I would force her to walk," the skinny auntie said.

They carried me inside, took off my new shoes and put me in bed.

"Now, child, have a rest. But you mustn't loosen the bandages or unwrap your feet, even during sleep. We'll be back tomorrow."

When I didn't say anything, the plump woman said, "Poor child. If you must, blame God for making you a girl."

The skinny one said, "Only girls with tiny feet can find a good *pojia*."

At my age, I already knew pojia means your husband's house.

"I don't want a pojia!" I said between sobs and crawled to the far corner of the bed.

"You silly little thing. Every girl needs a pojia. Even our empress dowager, Cixi, had a pojia. Her pojia was the emperor. Do you know that?" The plump auntie giggled. "One day you'll thank us for this."

Thank them? I wanted to scratch their faces.

My father and brothers returned in the afternoon. The boys looked at my feet, wide-eyed. Father put another box of green bean cakes on the table.

Upon seeing him, my tears gushed out like a river. "I don't want any cakes. I want my feet back."

Father sat down on the edge of my bed. "Now child, you mustn't say silly things. Without bound feet, no man will take you for a wife."

That night, I dreamed of falling into a pit full of mice with little red eyes. They swarmed over me and bit into my feet. I pulled them off by handfuls with my flesh still in their mouths.

When I awoke, my bandages were in disarray. I tried to rewrap my feet but couldn't.

The same aunties returned after my father left for work and my brothers went to their classroom in the courtyard. I shrank into the corner of the bed, up against the wall. "No! I don't want a pojia," I pleaded.

"Be a good girl," the skinny auntie dragged me out. When she saw the loose cloth dangling from my feet, she slapped my face hard.

"You good-for-nothing little thing! This will only make things worse."

The slapped cheek burned hot. Tears and snot smeared my face as I covered it with both hands, fearing another blow.

The plump auntie held me in her arms and soothed me. "Child, every girl must go through this. The more you fight, the more it'll hurt, and the longer it'll take for us to finish the job. You understand?"

As I sobbed, they rebound my feet tightly and put on my new shoes.

"Now walk!" the skinny auntie commanded.

They supported me from each side as I took a step. My knees buckled but they held me upright. After a few steps, I heard a pop and I collapsed. "My bone must be broken!" I howled. "Let me go! I beg you!"

They put me on the stool and unwrapped my feet. The white bandages were soaked with smelly blood.

The plump auntie picked up my new shoes and shook her head. "What a waste! I guess her father didn't know she would ruin them in no time."

They washed my feet with warm water, put alum powder between my toes and bound them even tighter. The bandage was twice the length of my body.

The skinny one said, "If you unwrap your feet again, you'll get a beating tomorrow. Now, your father left breakfast for you in the kitchen. Do you want it?"

I nodded. No point in fighting. Every girl had to go

through this. These two aunties also had bound feet themselves. There was no way out.

One auntie carried me back to my bed while the other went to the kitchen and brought back breakfast: boiled fine-dried noodles with chopped scallions, chili pepper, salt, vinegar, sesame oil and two poached eggs! I ate my food quietly while my tears fell into the bowl. I could hear my brothers reciting their lessons from the classroom. By my age, my brothers had begun schooling. After class, they would run, jump and climb trees and steal eggs from birds' nests. With my bound feet, I would never be able to do these things.

Despite the hell I went through, I failed to have the ideal three-cun golden water lilies because my father had put the whole foot-binding business off two years too long. The Hu clan blamed my father for his unforgivable delay. I could only blame God for making me a girl.

As I lay in bed in my new room, lost in thought, my husband walked in.

"I checked," he said. "There were no thorns on your seat or anywhere else."

I wanted to say someone must have removed them but stopped myself. What was I implying, that someone inside his family or among his guests had done it? I didn't want to be seen as a troublemaker on my wedding day.

"Forget about it," I said, but couldn't stop from wondering how a thirty-six-year-old man could have an adult son.

This is the moment. I closed my eyes and held my breath, expecting the worst—to be rejected because of my silver water lily feet.

Instead, I heard a gentle voice: "Do you feel better?"

I opened my eyes and saw him taking off his hat and unbuttoning his shirt. I averted my eyes.

"Yes, much better," I said in a whisper.

The next moment he was on top of me. I shut my eyes tightly, grasped the quilt and tried not to make a sound. Then a sharp pain, I knew I was no longer a maiden.

He cried out with the last thrust and rolled off me, totally spent. To my surprise, he kissed me gently on the cheek, seemingly to thank me.

It was over. Strangely, during the entire process, he didn't even glance at my feet, let alone play with them. Lying beside him, I figured this was perhaps a good time to ask about his son.

"I saw your son today," I said timidly.

"Yes. I didn't tell your father about him."

"How old is he?"

"Twenty-one."

"But you are only thirty-six."

"Actually, I'm forty-six," he said.

"But you told my father . . ." I couldn't believe what I was hearing.

"I was honest at first. I told the middleman my true age, but your father turned me down. So I subtracted ten years from my age, and it worked."

"It was you all along?" I was astonished.

"Yes." He grinned sheepishly.

"I thought your son had passed away."

"He did. But Qi is my other son."

"Your other son?" I was confused.

"He is an illegitimate child from a servant. First my wife

passed away, then my own son died. I had no one to continue my family line, so . . ."

"But you could have . . ." I trailed off, unsure of what to say next. He seemed to be able to read my mind.

"How could I? Most thirty-six-year-old men are not grandpas. Besides, I was ashamed." The grin faded from his face.

Not wanting to upset him, I reached out to his hand under the cover. After a moment, I asked, "Do they live here?"

"Yes, with their two-year-old son."

I had married a grandfather! Flabbergasted, I didn't know what to say. I felt cheated, but once rice is cooked, nobody can make it raw again. At least he seemed caring and had a successful business. As the saying goes, women marry men to be clothed and fed. For me, the most important thing was to have a family, to fill my house with the sounds of children's laughter.

Chapter 5

In my new home, my husband and I lived in the inner courtyard with my in-laws. Qi and his family lived in the outer courtyard. The day after the wedding, my husband and I dutifully went into the guest hall to greet my in-laws. The old couple sat at each end of the red wooden ba xian zhuo. My father-in-law was a little on the heavy side. My mother-in-law was thin with a yellow face. Neither of them smiled.

We bowed to my in-laws and sat on the chairs along the side. Qi and his wife were already seated.

"Golden Phoenix, I heard you fainted last night. What was the matter with you?" My mother-in-law's voice was ice cold.

"I . . . I . . ." *How did they know?* When I fainted, they both had left the banquet.

My husband came to my rescue. "Mother, it was very hot yesterday, and she had travelled a long way to get here. She's fine now."

"I thought country girls were tough. If we wanted a weakling to be our daughter-in-law, we would have chosen a city girl for our son. Li family relies on you to produce more boys. We hope you won't disappoint us."

"Yes, Mother." I bowed my head, not daring to look up.

"We heard you are a seamstress," my father-in-law said.

Before I could reply, my mother-in-law interjected, "In that case, you can take over the clothes-making for this family. Now we have a seamstress in our own home, why pay someone else to do the job?"

"Yes, Mother." I was not surprised. All daughters-in-law were servants.

"Grandmother," Pock-face chimed in. "Don't you want to test her cooking skills too?" She smiled sweetly.

"Of course." My mother-in-law brightened a little. "Why don't you cook lunch for us today?"

"Yes, Mother."

I made thin flatbreads for wrapping, stir-fried soybean sprouts and ground pork for stuffing, tomato and egg soup, and two cold dishes: chopped scallions mixed with *doufu*[7] and a cucumber salad—all simple everyday dishes. When the food was placed on the round dining table and the family of seven sat down, I had no idea if I would pass the test.

My mother-in-law bit into her wrap, closed her eyes and concentrated on chewing. My father-in-law tried a mouthful of the wrap as well.

"Good, very good indeed." The old man smiled for the first time. "What do you think, my son's mother?" he asked his wife.

She opened her eyes and nodded. "Not bad."

I let out a breath.

---

[7] *doufu*: Chinese spelling of tofu.

From that day on, I became the seamstress and cook for the entire family. I didn't mind cooking and sewing for my in-laws and my husband. But why should I do it for Qi and his wife? She was my daughter-in-law. She should serve me. When I brought this up to my husband, he said, "Do you know she is a terrible cook? Nobody likes her food. As for sewing, you are ten times—no, a hundred times—better than her."

"So the fast cattle get whipped?"

"I'm afraid so. Look, I feel sorry for you. However, they have a son. Their position is higher than yours in this family. Even Empress Dowager Cixi needed a son to gain power. As soon as you give me a son, things will change."

"If you wanted another son so much, why wait all these years to get married again?" In China, we believe in *duo zi duo fu*—the more sons, the more blessings. My husband had been a widower for many years.

"I was too busy building houses, and Qi never wanted me to remarry. He swore to look after me in my old age."

"Doesn't Qi want siblings? The more children you have, the more helping hands. Your business will only grow bigger."

"I have to admit, Qi is a selfish child. He and his wife want all the inheritance. Once more baby boys are born into the family, they'll have to share my estate."

By now, I was sure the thorns on my seat had been placed by these two wicked people.

"What made you change your mind?"

"Well, when I saw the opera costumes you made in the middleman's shop, I thought to myself, this is a woman worth having."

While I worried about the size of my feet all those years, in the end it was my skill that caught my husband's fancy.

Gradually, I learned my husband's story. Originally, his family name was not Li but Zhao, and his hometown was in Xin County, about three hundred *li*[8] away. He had no siblings. When he was seven, his family was robbed, and his father was kidnapped by bandits. When the family couldn't afford the ransom, the bandits *tore up the note*— they killed him.

The widow and son were too scared to live in the rural area. They travelled to Kaifeng to find a way to survive. When the last bit of money was gone, they begged on the streets. People pitied them. Someone in the neighbourhood suggested matching the beggar with the butcher, to find the poor mother and son a food bowl. The matchmaking worked. My husband became the stepson of Butcher Li, and his last name was changed accordingly.

Soon, the newlyweds had a son of their own, and the father showered all his love and affection on him, leaving none for the stepson. The father wouldn't allow little Haichun to go to school. The boy wanted to learn to read and write so badly that he found a job as a *book child* for a rich boy. His job was to prepare the student's writing paper and brush pen and to grind ink powder with water to make ink. During class, the book child needed to stand by to serve his master's every need. This was how my husband became literate. In the end, it was my husband—his stepson—who looked after and provided for the butcher

---

8 1 *li* = 0.5 kilometre

when he aged and retired, not his biological son, who had moved thousands of li away to Nanjing many years earlier.

How similar his story was to mine! My father hired a tutor to come to our house to teach Rui and Yu, but I was not allowed to set my feet in the classroom. However, whenever Father was away from home, I would put a little stool outside the classroom and listen in. How I loved the fragrance of the freshly ground ink. How I imagined the words taking shape on paper. The teacher pretended not to notice me, and my brothers ignored me. I learned the *Three-Character Canon* this way and could still recite it today:

> Man on earth,
> Good at birth.
> The same nature,
> Varies on nurture.
> With no education,
> There'd be aberration.
> To teach well,
> You deeply dwell.

> (人之初，性本善。性相近，习相远。苟不教，性乃迁。教之道，贵以专 ...)

If education is so important, why don't girls get any?

In the next few years, I eavesdropped on the classics such as *Lunyu* (*The Analects*), *Shijing* (*Book of Songs*) and the twenty-four stories of filial piety. Although I didn't understand everything I overheard and had nobody to ask questions, I did learn how to become a virtuous person.

Li Haichun began to make money for the family by peddling noodles in the street. Every morning, his mother would boil noodles, sprinkle on chopped scallions and cooked ground pork, pour *zhajiang* sauce onto the noodles and send him out with the pot.

One day, he tripped and dropped the noodle pot. Instead of panicking, the quick-thinking teen gathered the noodles back into the pot and ran home. There, the noodles were washed and re-boiled. Fresh scallions were sprinkled on, and zhajiang sauce was re-poured, and he was back out on the street again. Had his stepfather found out, there was no way he could escape a good beating.

When my husband grew into a young man, he found a secretarial job with a nearby county government. When he was laid off, he returned to Kaifeng and became a construction worker. He believed a big city could provide more opportunities than the countryside. Literate and smart, he was soon promoted to foreman. In this position, he learned how to estimate construction costs. Gathering a few friends, he started his own house-building business. Once the size and style of a house was determined, he could provide an accurate estimate of the number of bricks and roof tiles and the amount of lumber and clay needed. Gradually, he built up his reputation. When he saved up enough money, he stopped building houses for others and began to build them for himself. After a house was finished, if there was no immediate buyer, he would use it as collateral to finance his next house. This was called flipping tiles; thus, my husband became a tile flipper.

During the day, while my husband was out working, I laboured away, cooking and washing. After dark, when the entire family took a rest, I often sewed by oil lamp deep into the night. Whenever my mother-in-law saw the light in my room, she would yell from outside my window, "How much lamp oil have you brought to this family?" I soon learned to hang thick blankets on the windows after dark.

Five months into the marriage, my father came down with malaria. He asked a neighbour to send me a note. I asked my mother-in-law for a five-day leave to visit my father, but only got three. When I returned on the fourth day, I was ordered to kneel as a punishment. When my husband pleaded for leniency for me, he, too, was ordered to kneel. When bedtime came, my mother-in-law allowed her son to go to sleep, but not me. I knelt until dawn.

Once married, a woman was no longer free.

As the Chinese saying puts it, it is easier to be abused in the guest hall, that is, by your in-laws, than to be abused in your bedroom, that is, by your husband. At least my husband was kind to me. Once I gave birth to a son, I'd have nothing to worry about.

So I thought.

Chapter 6

God must have heard my prayers. A year later, I gave birth to a baby boy. We named him Zhong because we wanted him to be loyal to his country. My husband was ecstatic to finally have a legitimate son to carry on his family line. Required by tradition, I was in confinement for a month and most of the housework was assigned to Qi's wife and a newly hired maid. Since age twelve, this was the first time I could totally rest. My in-laws were also delighted to have another grandson and treated me better. Life couldn't be sweeter.

When little Zhong was one month old, we held the traditional one-month anniversary banquet to celebrate. I held my son high for all to see. Seeing Qi and his wife's sombre faces, I wanted to laugh out loud. When I came out of the confinement, I began to resist their demands. Now, Qi's wife had to do her own laundry and sewing.

One day, she came to my room, all smiles. "Ma, you are good at embroidery. Do you have some patterns I can borrow for pillowcases?"

"I haven't done it for a while. I'll have to find them."

People do change, I told myself.

Nobody was at home when I went over to Qi's quarter with a few patterns. Leaving the samples on their bed, I turned to leave. A sewing basket on the table caught my eye and I was curious to see her sewing skills. I lifted the cloth cover.

Lying in the basket was a hex doll with three shoe needles stabbed right through its heart. I picked it up and was stunned to see Zhong's name and date of birth written on the back. I dropped the doll like a piece of burning coal and ran to the door. Then I stopped. I couldn't let them harm my boy. I rushed back and pulled the needles out.

I must tell my husband. But what if he doesn't believe me? Just like the thorns incident, I need evidence. I took the doll and stumbled out of their room.

When I showed the doll to my husband that evening, he slammed his palm on the table with such force that the plates and bowls jumped. "That bastard!" He stormed out to the outer courtyard. I heard yelling, a crashing sound as an object hit the floor and Pock-face screaming. When he came back, his voice shook, "Let's move out of here."

The next day, my husband led me to his parents and presented the hex doll. Shocked, they questioned Qi and his wife who, in front of the hard evidence, couldn't deny it and knelt to my in-laws and my husband, asking for their forgiveness. My husband ignored them and told my in-laws that we were moving out. His parents pleaded, "We're old, and your brother lives far away. It's your duty to look after us."

When my husband didn't reply, the old butcher said, "If you absolutely cannot live with Qi under the same roof, let them move out."

My husband couldn't say no to that.

The perpetrators were ordered to move out. Pock-face

wailed, "We don't have a house. Where will we live? You don't want to chase us to the street, do you? After all, Qi is your own flesh and blood."

After a long silence, my husband said, "I've just finished building a property. You can move in there for now."

I knew my husband needed to sell the property to finance his next one, but I had no say in the matter. A wife was expected to always obey her husband.

Qi moved his family out at the end of the month to the new house. However, Pock-face didn't forget to leave the sliced embroidery patterns that I lent to her in their empty room for me to see.

"Once I make enough money," my husband vowed, "I'll build a big house for us. Sooner or later, we'll move out of here."

Meanwhile, in Shanghai, Yu had caused endless trouble by drinking excessively and gambling heavily. When he lost money, he often got into fights with other gamblers, and in the end, Rui had to pay Yu's debts for him. Eventually Rui sent Yu home. He had no place to go but to move in with my father. At least he can look after Father, I thought.

When Zhong was two years old, I gave birth to twin boys. We named them Wen and Wu—scholar and warrior. Even though Qi had moved out, I feared that evil couple might try to harm the newborns again. The hex doll trick had been used throughout history, including by the wives and concubines in emperors' harems, so it had to be harmful. However, if the date of birth on the doll was inaccurate, the curse wouldn't work, so we lied about the date and time of the twins' birth, even to the boys themselves. You never know what little children might reveal.

A year later, our daughter was born. We named her Xiuju—beautiful daisy. Since girls were not allowed to inherit assets, my daughter was safe, and we didn't have to lie about her birthday.

My mother-in-law died when Daisy was one. Then my father-in-law followed. He left his property to his biological son in Nanjing, even though my husband had built this house for them. I was only glad that we could finally move into the new house my husband had recently finished for us.

Our new complex contained six courtyards—three main yards and three side yards—all connected with twenty-eight rooms. The new house was located on Sunshine Street, with the entrance facing south, which, according to *fengshui* principles, would bring good energy into the complex. Three stone steps led to the front gate. Its one-*zhang*[9]-high double doors were lacquered dark red, with a corniced tile roof to protect the front gate from rain and snow. Each door had a brass knocker of a lion's face with a ring in its mouth. Inside the front gate was a tile-roofed screen wall, and in its centre, a carved dragon—eyes bulging, teeth bared and mane flying—riding clouds. It was believed that ghosts walk only in a straight line. Therefore, the screen wall with a dragon was sufficient to prevent them from entering the complex.

The main courtyard was the largest one. The most delicate side courtyard had a two-storey building with a cor-

---

[9] 1 *zhang* = 3.33 metres

niced roof and hardwood floor. The latticed windows were covered with paper. It also had a screen wall with a beautiful flying phoenix carved in the centre. I asked my husband what this courtyard was for.

"I don't know yet. I just wanted to build something nicer, fancier. It can be used as a study for our sons. I call it Phoenix Courtyard," he replied.

My name was Phoenix. Perhaps he used my name on purpose. Warmth spread through my body.

All the doors in our new complex were taller than average. My husband was so tall that he often had to bend to walk through a typical door. He didn't need to do so in his own home.

The middle side yard had a well and was the only area with bare ground and without any rooms. It was for our children to play in, my husband told me.

In the backyard was a hut and a tool shed for storage. A small corner gate opened to Cloth Street. Beyond that were the famous Lake Yang and Lake Pan, separated by a long dam from the north to the south but connected through an underground tunnel.

My husband planned to keep the principal courtyard and Phoenix Courtyard for our family and rent out the rest. The well yard was to be shared by all the residents. When my three sons grew up, they would each get a courtyard to live in.

"This way, we'll live all together and never be separated," my husband said.

So this would be our home for generations to come. With such a husband, I felt a sense of safety and security. He was a true protector of our family.

I grew to love this man.

Chapter 7

We moved into our new complex and rented out three courtyards as planned. The head of the first family was a rickshaw puller. The second was a shoemaker. The third was a blind fortune teller who was known in the neighbourhood as Blind Shen. After some discussion, we planted four fruit trees in the well yard—peach, date, apple and persimmon.

When Daisy was two years old, I gave birth to another girl we named Xiulan—beautiful orchid. We hired two nannies to help look after our two daughters while I cooked, washed and sewed. My boys had reached school age and started at the local public school. *With the protection of the dragon and the blessing of the phoenix, nothing bad would happen to us*, I told myself.

But bad things did happen.

When Yu couldn't repay his gambling debts again, he told his creditors they could have my father's house, where Yu and his wife still lived. By now, they had a girl, Primrose, and a younger boy, Tiger. The family of five had nowhere to go but my house. I couldn't refuse them, especially my father. My husband suggested we empty out the Phoenix Courtyard for them.

"That's the best yard." I wouldn't mind my father living there, but Yu didn't deserve it.

"We should always give the best to our guests, don't you agree?" my husband said.

I gave in, but with a condition: Yu must stop drinking. To my surprise, he agreed without a fuss. However, he didn't bother to find a job and soon his old habits returned. Whenever he wanted a drink, he sent my sons to a nearby restaurant to buy him wine and deep-fried peanuts. When he got drunk, he would smash wine cups and curse at the world.

My husband had stored a large pile of lumber in our backyard. One day, when he needed the lumber for a construction project, the pile was gone. His bottled-in frustration erupted.

"Your brother must have something to do with it. Just wait until he comes home!" he yelled.

Yu staggered into the courtyard, singing a tuneless melody. My husband stopped him in our courtyard. I heard loud arguing and ran out of the room in time to see Yu toss a stool at my children's father. He jumped aside, but Yu grabbed another stool. Before he could lift it, Orchid rushed at her uncle and sank her teeth into his forearm. Yu screamed, grabbed a handful of Orchid's hair and yanked. Blood instantly ran down my little girl's face. The hair had come off with a patch of skin. When we pried Orchid off her uncle, her mouth was bloody too.

Had I a knife in my hand, I would not have hesitated to kill my brother.

My husband screamed, "Get out! I never want to see you and your family again!"

This time, even Father couldn't plead for Yu. He and his family moved out, leaving my ailing father behind. We framed our brave little girl's hair and the patch of skin and hung it on our living room wall. With this artifact in plain sight, Yu would be too ashamed to enter our house again.

And he never did.

One fall day, a pale woman in black appeared at our doorstep. She was my brother Rui's wife, Pearl, who brought us the bad news—Rui had passed away. His heart just gave out and he died within hours. Pearl was here to carry out his last wish—to pass to my father his share of Rui's estate.

Father, Pearl and I shared stories about Rui. Pearl told us how Rui worked up from an accounting clerk position all the way to chief accountant, and how Rui came up with the money to settle Yu's gambling debts time and time again. I couldn't fathom how two brothers growing up in the same family could be so different. I told Pearl that when the two of them tried to catch sparrows, Rui watched the trap from behind a haystack all day long and Yu just waited to share the roasted birds. And when they tried to harvest dates from the trees, Rui would climb the tree to beat down the dates with a bamboo stick and Yu would stay on the ground to catch the fruit.

In the end, we all ran out of tears and words. Pearl left. The money Rui left for my father was enough to buy him a property. A month later, my husband found a nice little courtyard with five rooms. Within days of Father moving in, Yu and his family moved onto the new property as well.

I tried not to harbour my resentment toward Yu and focus on my own family.

My daughters were lucky that most city folks had abandoned foot-binding. My husband was fine with it, but his feminism only went so far. He wouldn't allow the girls to go to public school where the boys and girls were mixed. Although I was expected to obey him, I just couldn't let my daughters grow up illiterate, like me. The three of us resorted to a pretense—each morning, the girls waited until their father left for work, then they set off for school. In the afternoon, they left their bookbags at their friend's house before coming home, pretending they had been playing outside. We managed to keep the secret from my husband until his death.

I was proud of what I did. My daughters were literate and would become independent when they grew up. If they wanted to get married one day, it would not be for food and clothing but for love and to have families of their own.

Life handed me an even better deal.

As a Buddhist, my husband often attended services in Xiangguo Temple.

One day, he came home with a gentleman who looked to be in his late fifties, thin and pale, with white hair and a long beard. He wore a grey robe and seemed to carry an ethereal air. My husband introduced him as Mr. Ouyang, a friend he met in the temple.

From that day on, my husband often brought Mr. Ouyang home. All my children liked him and called him Uncle Ouyang. He was from a rich family and had several wives but no children. Obviously, money couldn't buy happiness. There were lots of fights, back-stabbing and power struggles among his wives. When Mr. Ouyang couldn't stand it anymore, he had left home, taking nothing but his painting brushes and a Chinese zither with twenty-one strings, to lead a vagrant's life.

I couldn't thank Buddha enough for our big, loving family; everyone was healthy, and we had enough money to live on.

Mr. Ouyang brought his zither to our home and played for us. The first piece was a happy tune. The music was so cheerful that the girls' faces opened like blossoming flowers. The boys were also transfixed.

After he finished, Orchid said, "Uncle Ouyang, one more, please."

Mr. Ouyang thought for a moment and restarted. This was a sad tune, like someone weeping. My heart trembled with the strings.

After he finished, we all fell silent. My husband knocked off the ash from his tobacco pipe. "Brother, you can't stay in the temple forever. Besides, you need someone to look after you. Come and live with us."

"Thank you for the offer. But—"

"No buts. It's decided." My husband stood up. "Our Phoenix Courtyard is perfect for you. The room on the first floor is big and bright. You can play the zither and paint there." He asked me to prepare the courtyard immediately and said to Mr. Ouyang, "Let's go get your stuff. You'll move in tonight."

My husband could be forceful sometimes.

Not only was Mr. Ouyang a very good musician, but he was also very good at Chinese watercolour painting. When he sold one piece of work, the money would last him a year. He took my three boys under his wing, teaching them to paint. Wen was the most diligent among the three. At mealtime, I always asked the boys to take one portion of our meal to Mr. Ouyang. We lived together like a family. My husband went so far as to offer Mr. Ouyang to choose one from our three boys as an adoptive son. After some hesitation, Mr. Ouyang chose Wen. A formal ceremony was held. We bought wine, and I cooked an eight-course meal with soup and rice. Wen ketoued to Mr. Ouyang three times and said, "Please accept me as your unworthy son, Father."

Both my husband and Mr. Ouyang got drunk that night. I was happy for Wen too.

Chapter 8

Two years flew by. Mr. Ouyang grew ill. He gifted Wen all his paintings, plus a few personal items, but instructed that the treasure could only be sold in case of financial emergency and hardship. This was beyond generosity.

In the winter of 1935, Mr. Ouyang passed away. Wen sat by his adoptive father's coffin to guard his spirit for seven days, even sleeping beside the coffin at night. A pimply rash spread over Wen's body. Dr. Cui, the local herbalist, told us it was an allergic reaction to the lacquer on the coffin. Still, Wen refused to leave the room until the week was over and it was time to bury Mr. Ouyang.

Wen became quieter and often stayed in the Phoenix Courtyard for hours, practising Chinese watercolour.

Then, my father took ill. On his deathbed, he held my hand and told me the years we worked together as a team were one of the happiest times of his life. After we buried him, Yu became the master of his house. Rui had worked so hard all his life but died young; Yu hardly worked at all but ended up owning the house bought with Rui's money. Where was the justice?

As a Chinese expression puts it, blessings do not come in pairs, and calamities never come alone. In January of 1936, only a few months after losing my father, my husband developed a high fever, his skin turned yellow and his lanky frame was soon all bones.

Dr. Cui diagnosed my husband with yellow jaundice.

Many packages of herbs later, there was no sign of recovery from my husband.

Each day, after the children had gone to school and I had fed my husband food and medicine, I often stood by the second-floor window of the Phoenix building, looking out to Lake Yang and Lake Pan. Everyone knew the stories of the loyal Yang family and the treacherous Pan family, who both served the emperors in the military for the Bei Song dynasty. Three generations of Yangs fought for the emperors of Song until only the twelve widows were alive. They took over their husbands' positions, leading their armies and defending their country against foreign military power. Mu Guiying was the most famous female warrior of them all. Back then, Lake Yang was owned by the Yang family, and Lake Pan by the Pan family. Mysteriously, the water in Lake Yang was always clear, and the water in Lake Pan was always muddy, even though they were connected by an underground tunnel.

On the street, newspaper boys shouted headlines about the Japanese troops' atrocities in Manchuria, northeastern China. Would they also invade the rest of China? With my husband by my side, I could face anything. I must restore his health.

It was a common belief that human flesh was the most powerful curative and could bring a very sick person back to life. When the fifth week had passed and my husband didn't get any better, I made the decision.

Waiting until all the children went to sleep, I sharpened a chopper and put a big bowl on the table alongside a piece of clean white cloth. Biting a chopstick, I positioned my left forearm above the bowl and held the chopper's wooden handle with my right hand. It shook uncontrollably. How I wished my father were here to wield the chopper for me!

I laid the cold, hard blade on my skin. The chopper shone in the lamplight. The blue veins under my dark skin stood out like little creeks. There was not much meat, just muscle, toughened up from years of hard work. Would it be tasty? When I was six, I suffered foot-binding for my future husband. Now, at age forty-four, I was willing to feed my flesh to him. There was love, and there was the cold fact that, without him, I didn't think the children and I could survive.

The clock chimed. I looked up. It was late. I had to do this.

I sliced the skin with one quick motion. Blood gushed out but the meat was still attached to my arm by a patch of skin. The chopper fell from my slippery hand, narrowly missing my right foot. The pain was excruciating. *Don't faint! You must finish what you started*, I told myself and picked up the chopper with a shaking hand. This time it seemed more difficult than the first strike. I bit into the chopstick like a vice and cut through the attached skin. A patch of meat fell into the bowl, along with blood and my salty tears. I bit hard on the chopstick, wrapped the wound tight with the cloth, and used my right hand and teeth to tie a knot. Blood oozed under the bandage.

The worst was over. I picked the lump up by my thumb and index finger and quickly tossed it in the boiling water, then closed my eyes, fighting hard not to throw up. I had done it, even though the veins in that arm throbbed and threatened to burst open.

The next morning, I placed the soup bowl on the edge of the bed and spoon-fed my husband the soup with my right arm.

"What's this?" my husband asked weakly.

"Pork soup," I lied.

"It's so tender."

Feeling the bandage inside my loose shirt sleeve, I said, "It's from a piglet. I got it especially for you."

After he laid back down, he sighed, "Golden Phoenix, I'm not sure if I'll recover—"

"Don't say that. It'll bring bad luck. You'll get better. You will."

He closed his eyes for a moment and reopened them. "There's something I must tell you. Besides our house, I also bought ten mu of reed marshland. It's located just south of the city." He drew a breath. "It's dirt cheap. I bet one day it will go up in value. Don't let anyone sell it until then."

I understood that "anyone" meant our sons. As a wife, I had no right to inherit any of his properties.

I nodded.

"My clothing trunk has a double bottom with a secret chamber. All the deeds are hidden there, including the one for this house." He stopped to catch his breath. "The deed for the house that I lent to Qi is there too, but

I'm afraid you can't get that one back." He took another break. "If you can rent all four courtyards out, including the Phoenix Courtyard, you should be able to manage."

"Don't say such things." I forced out a smile. "Tomorrow I'll go to Xiangguo Temple to ask Buddha for help."

"Also," he continued, ignoring my words, "the world is very troublesome. It's the time for which you and the children need me the most, but I have to go."

Tears burst out from my eyes. I told myself not to cry in front of my husband, but couldn't stop it. "Please, don't talk like this anymore. I can't bear it." I reached over to grab his hands, forgetting about my wounded arm. The sharp pain made me almost cry out.

Oh please, lao tian ye,[10] *please do not let my husband die. I'll do anything to save him. I'll cut off my entire arm if I have to. Just show me the way.*

"You must promise me to keep the children alive and pass this house to our sons when they grow up."

I noticed he used the word "alive." By then, the Japanese troops had occupied Manchuria for five years, and they could invade the rest of China at any time. Once a war broke out, nobody was safe. Still, I said, "I promise."

---

[10] *lao tian ye:* god, generally, not a specific god

Chapter 9

I was counting on my sacrifice to save my husband's life. But in the end, God still took him away before my wound had healed. Was my sacrifice not big enough? Had I not prayed hard enough? When my children asked me what was wrong with my arm, I feared they would question my sanity, but I didn't know how to lie either. In the end, I explained that I just had to try everything and didn't want to have any regrets. The boys didn't say anything. Asking if I was in pain, Daisy offered to help me with cooking. I cleaned and dressed the wound every night. A visit to a herb store taught me to use plantain to prevent infection.

I put my husband's corpse in a black coffin and turned our reception hall into a mourning place. A portrait of him hung on the wall facing the door, along with my children's mourning wreath. The children read the couplets to me that Wen had written on their wreath: "Kindness, unforgettable and true, Family bond, forever in view. Inheriting the legacy with pride, Praising the departed who bravely died." (难忘手泽，永忆天伦，继承遗志，克颂先芬.)

My late husband's friends and employees also sent their respects. Their funeral scrolls, written with commendable couplets, were hung on either side of the wreath and portrait. I asked my children to read them to me: "The voice and figure now unseen, yet virtue's light still brightly gleams. The Spirit lives on, never to fade, Style forever, a legacy made." (音容已杳，德泽犹存。精神不死，风范永存.) "The life of frugality to set an example, Half a century of hard work, a legacy ample." (一生俭朴留典范，半世勤劳传嘉风.) "Throughout life, do good deeds without rest, A name that will live on, one of the best." (一生行好事，千古流芳名.)

On the table underneath the portrait, a pair of white candles burned day and night. Different kinds of sweet buns and dried fruits were offered to his spirit; fresh fruits were the best, but in winter they were not available. A clay jar for burning paper money was placed before the table, and a guiding light hung at the head of the coffin for the departing soul.

People believed that on the third day after a death, the soul of the departed would return to visit his family and loved ones. Therefore, by tradition, my three boys and I kept a vigil beside the coffin for three days. It also gave relatives and friends enough time to pay their final respects and offer their condolences. We kept our front gate open all day long for the visitors.

Qi and his wife showed up on the first day. Even though I never liked these two, I had to allow them to pay respect to their deceased father. After they ketoued three times in front of the deceased's portrait, Qi asked me where I planned to bury his father.

I was puzzled. "In Li's family cemetery, of course."

"I see." Qi didn't say anything more, and they left.

On the second day, just after lunch, a stranger walked

in. He was one head taller than me, fat as a pig, with bulging eyes like a frog's, a wide meaty nose and a paunch.

"My name is Li Xicai. People called me Big Grandpa Li. We are family. Do you know that?"

"No." I was startled by his declaration.

He ignored my frown. "I'm sorry that your husband passed away. Since we are family, I'm entitled to half of his estate. Do you know that?"

What? A total stranger showed up in our house before my husband's body had turned cold, demanding half of his estate. I had heard a widow was often a target for extortion, but never expected it would happen to me, and so quickly. My heart beat like a drum, but I could not let him sense my fear.

I raised my voice: "I don't know you, and I have nothing to give you. Besides, my husband's real last name was Zhao. He only changed his family name when his mother married Butcher Li. Therefore, you and I are not related at all!"

"I see. Since you said your husband's real last name was Zhao, you can't bury him in Li's family cemetery. I'll dig his corpse out if I must. So either we share his estate, or I leave your husband's body for dogs. It's up to you."

"Get out!" Zhong shouted.

The thug pointed his finger at us before he left. "This isn't the end of the matter. I'll be back."

Wu shut the door behind him with a bang. Wen, knuckles white, helped me to a chair. Daisy was in tears, and Orchid said, "Ma, don't be afraid. We will protect you."

"Who is this person? How did he know our last name?" I asked my sons.

Wen said, "Ma, do you think it has something to do with Qi? Remember, yesterday Qi asked about my father's intended burial place."

Wen was right. I couldn't think of any other reason for this man to show up like that. It had to be that bastard!

"I heard that one can lease a burial spot in another cemetery," Zhong said. "Would you consider that?"

"Let me think about this." Leasing a burial space meant placing the coffin on the surface and covering it with a brick shell—making it easy to remove when the lease is up—not an ideal way to bury a loved one. But it would be better than letting my husband's body be dug up and left for dogs. My poor husband. He'd worked so hard all his life building houses for others. In the end, he couldn't even own a hole in the ground. "But what if they hear about this and cause trouble at the leased place?"

"We can't let Qi find out the burial day, so we can't invite any friends," Wen said. "We must keep it a secret."

I had to agree. That also meant I couldn't hire trumpeters and professional mourners.

On the fourth day, we put my husband's coffin on a hired horse cart. My children and I rode in a second horse cart and left home before dawn. I brought paper money to burn at his gravesite for use in the other world.

We first headed to the Li family burial ground. Then, at the planned spot, we made a sharp turn and headed in a different direction. I figured by the time my stepson found out our plan, it would be too late to intercept us.

When the coffin was placed on the ground, the four workers hired to build the grave began to work.

"Stop! Stop!" I turned and saw Qi and the tyrant who claimed to be my husband's heir rush toward us, followed by two thugs. All four waved long sticks and scowled at us. An invisible hand seized my heart. Despite our careful planning, they'd found us! I placed my hands on Wen's and Wu's shoulders for support.

The leader of the hired workers, a tall, strong young man in his twenties, stood up straight, still holding his shovel. "What's the matter?"

"This is a family matter," sneered Qi. "You must stop this immediately."

The young man tightened his grip on the shovel and glanced at me over his shoulder. "Get the children in the cart."

We scrambled in and crouched down, but Wu stood with a slingshot in his hands.

"No!" I snatched it away and pulled him down. I didn't want the cemetery to become a war zone.

"You can discuss your family business after the burial," the leader said. "We are hired workers. We must finish our job."

"The dead man is my father. We will discuss our family matter right now!" Qi shouted.

Standing with arms akimbo and legs apart, the tyrant echoed, "Yes, we must discuss it right now."

"What kind of son won't let his father rest in peace? Shame on you!" The leader raised his voice and pointed the shovel at the tyrant. "I know you. You have been bullying the neighbourhood for years. Now you are trying to take advantage of a widow. Fight me if you wish." Behind the leader, the other workers raised their shovels as well.

The tyrant hesitated. Before I could stop them, Zhong, Wen and Wu jumped off the cart and picked up some bricks.

"Go away!" Zhong screamed. "You bastard!" Wen and Wu stood beside their big brother, staring down their enemies.

Qi hesitated for a moment, then yelled at me, "You wait. One day, I'll settle this with you!"

They took off.

The gravediggers were strangers to our family, and yet they had risked their lives protecting us. I would never forget it, and I told my children to always remember these good-hearted people.

After my husband's passing, our family relied on rental income to survive. I thought of reopening my sewing business but cooking and washing for the family of six took all my time; the rent barely made ends meet. Fortunately, Zhong had only one school year left. Once he graduated, he could work to subsidize the family.

July 8, 1937, began just like any other day. I cooked breakfast for my children. After eating, they all set off for school. I finished washing the dishes and went to the well yard to pick some peaches. They were big and juicy, and I planned to give some to my renters.

The high-pitched shouts of newspaper boys arose in the street: "Extra! Extra! The Japanese attacked the town of Wanping County! The Chinese army fights to the last drop of blood to defend Wanping County and Marco Polo Bridge. Extra! Extra! . . ."

I rushed to my front gate. The shoemaker and the fortune teller, Blind Shen, also came out.

The shoemaker bought the newspaper. Blind Shen and I gathered around him.

"What does it say?" I asked anxiously.

He opened the newspaper and read, "Marco Polo Bridge Incident. In the middle of last night, the Japanese army conducted a military exercise near the Marco Polo Bridge, southwest of Beiping. They claimed a soldier of theirs was missing and demanded a search in the Town of Wanping County. The defending Chinese Twenty-ninth Army refused. The Japanese army launched an attack with machine guns and bombed the Town of Wanping. Countless people died, and many more were wounded."

I asked Blind Shen, "How far is Macro Polo Bridge?"

"Over three thousand li away."

"Can our army withstand the attack?"

"I hope so." The old man lifted his sightless eyes toward the sky. "Jade Emperor in Heaven, please protect our soldiers. Protect our country."

Relying on the Jade Emperor? Yes, he blessed me with three sons. But when my father and my husband were gravely ill, my prayers seemed to fall on deaf ears. Would he protect our land and our people? I was no longer sure.

When my children came home at lunchtime, they told me they had learned about the attack at school.

"Ma, our school will protest against the Marco Polo Bridge incident tomorrow," Zhong said.

"Our school too," Wen and Wu said.

"Can we join you?" Daisy and Orchid asked.

"Of course not," Zhong said.

I didn't mind the boys participating in such activities, but my girls were obviously too young.

The newspaper boy brought bad news to us every day. On July 29, 1937, our capital, Beiping, fell into the enemy's hands. One day later, the nearby coast city of Tianjin fell.

On August 13, the Japanese shelled Shanghai with tons of bombs. The Chinese army defended the city for ten days but eventually lost it.

China was in a state of emergency. Facing a common enemy, the Nationalists and Communists had joined forces for the second time, but rumours about the Communists' intention to communize properties and women had never ceased. Why would the Nationalists want to join forces with them?

By the fall, the war between the Japanese and the Chinese armies raged in our neighbouring province, Shanxi. More and more people left their homes and fled to the west. By October, the shoemaker and the rickshaw puller ended their leases. When the fortune teller told me his family was leaving too, I was truly scared.

But we couldn't leave. My girls were too young. Besides, where would we go? My husband had told me that as long as I kept the house, our family would be fine.

I must trust him.

Chapter 10

With no rental income, we began to sell furniture, a few pieces at a time. First, the console table. Then my favourite tea tables and matching chairs. After that, eight datewood armchairs. Finally, I had to part with the bureau. Only the dining table and a few stools were left, along with the trunk that held my husband's clothing. I could never sell that because it hid the property deeds.

When most of the furniture was gone, we began to taste starvation.

One day, I sent Wen to the noodle shop owned by Lumpy Head. The shopkeeper had received his nickname after falling from a ladder and sustaining an injury to his skull. I asked Wen to buy one pound of green bean noodles—the only type we could afford—on credit. When Wen returned, he told me that Lumpy Head had turned him away and continued to serve other customers. Wen had stood beside the till until the last customer left the store. Reluctantly, Lumpy Head measured out one pound of green bean noodles and said to Wen, "You haven't paid for the previous time. Next time you are here, I expect payment before selling you anything on credit again. Make sure you tell your mother."

I cooked the noodles with plenty of water to make the food stretch as much as possible. By the time the noodle soup was on the table, we all wept.

Wen finally stopped crying. "If we stay here, we'll starve to death."

"Where can we go?" I blew my nose, never having felt so helpless.

Wen and Wu exchanged a look.

"What is it?" I demanded.

Wu fiddled with his hands, then looked at me. "Wen and I plan to join the Eighth Route Army."

"What Eighth Route Army?" I was alert.

"They were the old Red Army." The words coming from the lips of my son made me stiffen.

"Aren't they the Communists? They are gangsters!" I cried out.

"They are not!" Wu also raised his voice.

"Shh . . ." Wen put his index finger against his own lips, then turned to me.

"Mother, that's how the Nationalists slander the Communists."

"But haven't they joined forces now?" I got more confused.

Wu took over. "Yes, but the Nationalists were forced to join forces with the Communists, only because Chiang Kai-shek[11] was kidnapped by his own General Zhang Xueliang during the Xi'an incident last December. The Nationalists never like the Communists."

---

[11] Chiang Kai-shek, also known as Jiang Jieshi or Jiang Zhongzheng (1887–1975), was a key ally of Sun Zhongshan, the leader of the Kuomintang (KMT—the Chinese Nationalist Party) and was the Republic of China's political and military leader.

Wen shushed Wu to lower his voice, then said, "Mother, the Communists fight for justice and equality between men and women, between rich and poor, between the powerful and the powerless. The Eighth Route Army is the people's army. The Communists are the new hope for China!"

Wu chimed in, "Look at us. After Father died, we became poor overnight. We're bullied by Qi, and there's no one we can turn to for help. You can't take over Father's business because you're a woman. This is not right. It's not fair. So many Chinese are robbed and killed by bandits and warlords. There's no peace in China. We must fight for our rights and our lives."

Rights—what a strange word. Ever since I was a little girl, I knew only of my duties and obligations. I'd never thought of my rights.

"What rights?" I asked nobody in particular.

"The right to be alive; the right to be treated as a human being; the right to own properties, to go after what you want in life. To be free." Wen's face glowed with hope and determination.

"But you're so young! You have no military training. You haven't even finished school yet." I was half-commanding, half-begging. I had already lost my parents, my brother Rui and my husband. I wouldn't send my boys to the battlefields to be killed!

Wen sat a bit straighter. "The enemy is coming. If we do nothing, the Japanese will take the rest of China, just as they took over Manchuria in 1931. They will kill our people and burn our houses. How can we wait any longer?"

"Ma, don't worry. We'll receive training." Wu put his arm around Wen and shook Wen's shoulder lightly.

Zhong spoke for the first time. "If you want to fight the Japanese, you can join the Chinese National Revolutionary Army right here in Kaifeng."

I gave Zhong a look. He was not helping.

Wen said, "We're underage. The Nationalist Army won't take us."

Zhong arched his eyebrows. "And the Communists will?"

"Yes. They take everyone—women, children, rich, poor." Wu grinned as if this was a game.

Orchid blurted out, "I want to join the Eighth Route Army too."

"When adults talk, don't interrupt." I shot Orchid a look only to realize that both Wen and Wu were still children.

I said to the twins, "It's dangerous! You two are only sixteen. I won't let you."

"Do you want us to starve to death?" Wu challenged.

Indeed, if the twins remained home, how could I feed them.

"How will you get to Shanbei? It's a long way." I tried to put as many barriers as possible in front of them.

"We will take a train to Xi'an. The Eighth Route Army has set up recruiting booths in the city. All we need is to find such a booth. Then we will be transferred to northern Shaanxi," Wen said.

"How do you know all this?" I was surprised.

"From our mentor in school," Wu said rather proudly.

I didn't need to ask further. I had heard about underground Communists. They were certainly doing a good job.

"Let me think this over," I finally said.

That night, after we all went to bed, someone banged on our front gate. Was it a neighbour in urgent need of help?

I jumped out of bed, lit the lamp and dressed quickly. The children also got up. Together, we opened the front door.

Standing there was Qi, now sturdy and darker, in a brown uniform. He held a handgun and smiled menacingly. "I went to Shandong and joined Warlord Han Fuju's army. I'm on leave."

Before I had a chance to say anything, he fired a shot toward the sky. Daisy shrieked. She and Orchid hid behind me, gripping the hem of my clothes. I put a hand on my chest involuntarily, trying to calm my pounding heart.

"You have one month to move out from my father's property. If you refuse, I'll lead my fellow soldiers to your house, seize your property and take your sons away." He fired another shot into the air before walking away.

My entire body shook. Zhong took the lamp from my unsteady hand.

"Ma, don't you see?" Wen said earnestly. "We need guns to defend ourselves and to fight for our rights and our lives."

"This is not a good place to talk. Let's go inside." I led the children back into the house, and we sat down around the dining table.

"Let them go, Mother," Zhong said. "At least they won't starve. I'll look after you and my sisters."

I had no choice. Wen and Wu were right. Women and children were always powerless and helpless. I could lose everything. I looked at my twins. They were so young and yet so determined. I wanted to touch their cheeks, maybe for the last time. No, I couldn't think like that. But I was not used to expressing my emotions this way. I clenched my hands on my lap and forced myself not to cry.

"Fine," I finally said, "but not before I make you two each a new winter jacket and a new pair of shoes."

The next day, I went through our old clothes and salvaged enough material. Zhong took over the job of cooking. I stayed in my own room, concentrating on my project.

The weather turned cold and the trees were bare. The night before the twins left, we wrapped the treasures Mr. Ouyang had left for Wen in oil paper, hid them in a huge clay jar and sealed the lid with wax. We removed some bricks from our storage room floor, dug out a pit and buried the jar. We restored the bricks, making sure no marks remained, and piled up junk on top of it. This was our emergency fund, our last resort.

The boys left home secretly. Wu got to the train station first. Wen and I pretended we were on our way to visit relatives out of town. I carried a basket filled with Chinese chives as a gift to our relatives, in case someone we knew got nosy, and we went to the train station to join Wu.

When the train carried my boys away, tears finally ran down my face. Within a year and a half, Rui, Mr. Ouyang, my father and my husband were all gone. Now I had sent my teenage sons to the battlefields. How much more sorrow could I endure? I lifted my face to the sky and said involuntarily, *Oh, Jade Emperor, if you are really there, please protect my sons. Please let them live.*

Chapter 11

Shortly after the twins left home, I found another tenant; Mrs. Lin, a childless widow living off her husband's small inheritance. She took a room and a kitchen in the front courtyard. The rental income was barely enough for me to put food on the table, but it was better than nothing.

In the early spring of 1938, when the Spring Festival was just over, a dark-skinned, skinny teenage boy came to my door. Dirty and in shabby clothes, hair long and unkempt, he reminded me of a scarecrow. His face turned red before he opened his mouth, "I'm here to look for my aunt."

"What's your aunt's name?"

"Golden Phoenix."

I took a close look at him. "It's me, but who are you."

"My mother was Golden Lotus."

My goodness! Golden Lotus was my cousin. At age sixteen, she married a farmer far away in Gao Village, Xiayi County. The last time I saw her was shortly after I was married. She and her husband came to Kaifeng to visit us and talked about adopting a child because after ten years of marriage, they failed to produce a child of their own. This boy had to be their adopted son.

"My goodness! I *am* your aunt. Your name?"

"Stone. I finally found you!" The boy dropped on the ground and ketoued to me.

I was taken aback and pulled him up in a hurry. "What're you doing? Come inside."

Once we were seated in my guest hall, I asked, "How are your parents?"

Tears gushed out and left dirty marks on his dusty face. "Killed."

What? I couldn't believe my ears and waited for him to continue. When nothing came out of his mouth, I asked, "How?"

"By bandits." After that, he wept silently. So he was a boy with few words.

I stood up. "I'll get water for you to wash up. You must be hungry too. I'll cook something for you."

After he washed his face, cleaned his hands and wolfed down three bowls of noodles, we settled in the guest hall and started the conversation again. Since all my children were in school, it was just the two of us. Still he said little, answering my questions with only a few words. When I stopped, he stopped. Finally, piece by piece, I learned what had happened to his parents.

One night, after the family had gone to sleep, they heard shouting outside, warning that bandits were coming.

"Go hide!" his father urged Stone before going to the courtyard. His mother followed his father. Stone hid under his bed and heard their front door smash open and the sound of horses' hooves, footsteps, the clatter of metal and shouting. His father begged the bandits to leave them alone because they didn't have anything worth taking. The bandits ordered his father to shut up and they searched the house. Then Stone heard his father screaming, "Not the grain seeds! I'd rather die." The robbers laughed, then a gunshot. His mother screamed. Another gunshot. The screaming stopped abruptly.

When it was quiet down in the courtyard, Stone crept out only to find his parents' bloody corpses.

My poor cousin. We all knew bandits roamed the rural areas, but it was still a huge shock that they killed my relatives. I handed over a handkerchief to the boy. By now my own face was covered by tears as well.

"Who buried your parents?" I asked.

"The uncles and aunties in our village."

"How did you find me?"

"My mother told me you moved to Kaifeng when you married," he said.

"And? . . ." I prompted.

"I set off for Kaifeng."

"How long has it taken you to get here?"

"Two weeks. No, three weeks. No, twenty-one days."

I almost laughed. Twenty-one days and three weeks are the same thing. Obviously, his mind was not clear. But after witnessing such a horrific event, I didn't blame him.

"But how did you know where I live?"

"I didn't."

Carrying on this conversation was too hard. Getting things out of his mouth was like squeezing out toothpaste from a tube. But I told myself I must be patient.

"Then how—?"

"I went to Xiangguo Temple to beg. The monks there let me sleep on a veranda at night. I helped them with chores, and was allowed to stand at the end of the line at mealtime."

When I saw he had no intention of continuing, I prompted him again, "Then . . . ?"

"I told them I was looking for you. They asked your husband's name. I told them. An old monk told me he knew my uncle, dead now. He also knew where you lived."

"How have you survived on the way here?"

"Begged." Suddenly, without my asking a question, he blurted out, "May I stay?"

"Of course," I said. "Which grade are you at in school?"

"No school." Stone lowered his head, then added, "I can work." This was the second time he said something on his own.

"Don't worry about that yet," I said.

Stone told me he was born in the year of the dog—the same year Zhong was born. That made him eighteen in the lunar calendar but only seventeen in the Western calendar. I didn't think he knew he was adopted because my cousin would have kept it a secret. People believed if a child knew he was adopted, he would never bond with his adoptive parents. When he grew up, he would run away to find his biological parents.

An illiterate boy had fewer job choices. I went to Mrs. Lin for advice. She said a restaurant nearby was looking for an apprentice. The next day, I took Stone there. The restaurant owner, Master Chen, was a short round man with a pale complexion. He almost rolled out from the kitchen. When he learned why we were there, he asked Stone, "What's your name?"

"Stone."

"How old are you?"

"Eighteen."

"Ever cooked before?"

"No."

Master Chen said to me, "At least he is honest. I need an apprentice at the breadboard. He doesn't get paid. But he can eat three meals in the restaurant."

I knew "breadboard" in restaurants had everything to do with wheat flour, such as noodles, buns, dumplings, baozi, flatbreads, pies, pastries and pancakes. Since we lived in northern China, most of our food was made of wheat flour. Stone could learn a lot. I thanked Master Chen profusely. Stone said nothing, only bowed to his new boss.

Master Chen smiled. His eyes became two thin lines, making him look like a Buddha.

Master Chen turned out to be a Buddha. When he found out about our financial situation, he allowed Stone to bring home leftovers from the restaurant.

Also, I heard Qi had gone back to Shandong in a hurry, to Warlord Han's army. Without that wicked man around, I could sleep better at night. Still, I feared one day he would suddenly show up at our front door and kick us out of our own home.

Stone was content to have three meals a day and a roof above his head. At home, he didn't talk much but always did what he was told, even when orders came from the girls. He never complained either. However, sometimes he could be absent-minded and forgetful. For example, he forgot to lock the front door after dark more than once. Also, there was the time when I asked him to fetch water from the well, and he failed to return. I went to look for him, only to find him sitting on the well platform, crying. It turned out it was his job back at home to fetch water from the village well for his parents. There were also times when I asked the boy to take the clothes off the clothesline; he would stop midway, staring at the garments, which must have reminded him of his mother. Sometimes I caught him in a daze, not aware of what was going on around him. When startled by a sudden sound or movement, he seemed to be awakened from a trance. The poor child had suffered the most horrific trauma of his life and needed time to recover.

With all that good food, however, Stone was no longer a scarecrow. He grew half a head taller than Zhong and three times thicker and somehow looked familiar. That was strange because the boy obviously didn't have my cousin's looks. It was his eyes, his manners and the way he walked and gestured. His biceps bulged from kneading dough all day long. I didn't have enough money to make new clothes so I altered my late husband's old clothes to fit him, just as I did for Zhong. Having two boys at home, especially one strong like Stone, made me feel safer. Ever since the twins left home, I had not received a word from them. Stone filled the empty hole in my heart, and my affection for him grew. I treasured this feeling and didn't want to lose the boy. So one day I said to him, "If you don't mind this poor woman, be my son."

He nodded. But this was a big thing for both of us. Merely nodding was not enough for me. I asked him again. He blushed and said yes. I asked Zhong to check the almanac for the next auspicious day for the ritual. On that day, I handed Stone a bowl, a pair of chopsticks and a new shirt that I had made for him. He knelt on the floor and said, "Mother, please accept your unworthy son's curtsy," then ketoued three times to me. From that moment, I had a fourth son, and I changed his name from Stone to Xiao, meaning filial piety. This was the name my husband and I had wanted for our second son, but I gave birth to the twins, and we named them Wen and Wu. In Chinese legendary storytelling, a scholar and a warrior usually work side by side in their adventure.

My family of six had dropped to four when the twins left home. Now it had grown to five. All I needed was to keep it together and make sure no harm came to my children. Once they grew up and got married, my family would expand again.

The Japanese troops were closing in, and half the city was empty. I didn't know what to do because I didn't want to leave our house, but I also knew we may have to. I bundled up two sets of clothes for each of us and sewed the small amount of cash I had inside of a money belt that could be wrapped around my waist. We'd be ready to flee at the last moment. I asked Mrs. Lin if she would go with us.

"I'm already sixty-one, with bound feet, how far can I run?" she sighed.

"What if they bomb Kaifeng?" I asked.

"If I must die, let it be. I'm not going anywhere," was her answer.

Japanese Occupation

KAIFENG CITY–
LUOYANG CITY–KAIFENG CITY

1938–1945

Chapter 12

May 23, 1938, was a day I would never forget. Kaifeng sweltered under the merciless sun. Sweat covered my face, forehead and neck as I cooked. I was making crepes and stir-fried soybean sprouts for spring rolls, my children's favourite food. The proper stuffing for spring rolls should always include ground pork, which we couldn't afford. When supper was ready, I waited for my three children to return from school and Xiao to return from work.

First Zhong arrived. I heard him before I saw him.

"Ma, I'm back. Starving to death," he said as he came to the kitchen and stretched his neck over the wok. "On my way home, I saw many more people leaving town. Perhaps we should leave too."

"I don't know." I had trouble sleeping at night and flinched at every loud sound. We had discussed leaving for days. The government had deserted Kaifeng and the Nationalist troops were nowhere in sight. When the enemy was about to attack us, the civilians were left with no protection and no weapons to defend themselves. We didn't have relatives in the countryside or in our neighbouring province to give us food and shelter. With my deformed feet, I would become a burden to my children. But staying was even more dangerous. Rumours of the Japanese Three All policy—burn all, kill all and loot all—had travelled far ahead of their troops. One wrong decision could mean lost lives. It was so hard to be the only parent. I had no one to discuss the issue with or to rely on.

Soon, Xiao came home, bringing some leftovers from the restaurant as usual.

The sky bruised to pink and purple, and gradually gave in to darkness. The girls hadn't returned.

"Let's eat," Zhong suggested. "We can save some for them."

"Fine," I finally said.

When we finished eating, the girls still had not returned.

"Something must have happened." A block of tangled hemp twines seemed to fill my chest.

Xiao wiped his mouth with the back of his hand, even though I told him many times to use a handkerchief. "Maybe their rehearsal is running late."

Both Daisy and Orchid had been selected for admittance into the city's Children's Performing Arts Group a few months earlier, and they had been busy rehearsing anti-war, anti-Japanese shows.

I asked Zhong to go look for them. Half an hour later, he came back alone and told us the school was empty.

"How about the rehearsal hall? Did you go there?" I asked.

"Yes, I did. It was empty too."

My legs felt like they were made of dough. I clutched the edge of the table to prevent myself from falling.

"People are leaving the town. Maybe they left with their school or the art group," Zhong suggested.

"But they should have come home to tell us, or at least sent a note." Then I remembered Primrose, my brother Yu's daughter. She was also a member of the performing arts group. Even though I hadn't talked to my brother for years and had no intention of ever seeing him again, I had to go to him. "Zhong, I need to go to your Uncle Yu. Come with me."

My father's house was now Yu's home. Four and a half city blocks later, I knocked on his door.

Yu hadn't changed much, other than the deepened wrinkles on his face. "It's you?" After that, he forgot to close his mouth.

"Has Primrose come home from school?" I was not in the mood for small talk.

"No, she hasn't." He hesitated, then stepped aside. "Come in, please."

"No need. Aren't you worried about her?"

The corners of his mouth dropped. "Of course I am."

"Is it possible that the performing arts group has left the city?" My voice was flat.

"Maybe." His eyes lost focus.

"What do you plan to do? Leave or stay?" I regretted the moment I said this. His decision had nothing to do with mine.

"Don't know."

There was a possibility that my girls might have fled the city with the group, and the teachers were there to look after them. If we stayed, we might get ourselves killed. But what if the girls were still in Kaifeng? What if they came home, and we were gone? I could never live with myself.

That night, I twisted and turned. When I finally fell

asleep, I dreamt of my girls. We were climbing a mountain. Then they both slipped away on a steep slope. I reached out to them but only managed to grab a handful of Orchid's shirt. I woke up panting, holding the edge of my bedroll in a death grip.

The following day, Zhong's school was shut down. The teachers urged everyone to leave the city. Master Chen also locked up the restaurant and sent Xiao home. We could hear bombing in the distance and watched people rushing out of the city like a tidal wave.

We waited.

The next morning, we awoke to a blazing hell. An ear-piercing racket filled the air. Airplanes flew low and bombs rained down like hailstones. Houses and buildings burned, and black smoke rose to the sky.

"Ma, we have to run," Zhong yelled.

Zhong was right. We had been preparing for this moment for weeks. I quickly fastened the money belt around my waist. Zhong slung the clothes bundle on his shoulder. Xiao stuffed four steamed buns in the pockets of his trousers. As we rushed past Mrs. Lin's room, I shouted through her open window, "We're leaving, you can still come with us!"

Mrs. Lin stuck her head out and waved at us. "You go along. I'll watch the house for you."

"May Buddha protect you!" I shouted, and we crossed the doorsill of our front gate. Just as I was about to close it behind me, Zhong cried out, "Wait!" and ran back into the house. He came out with a green quilt.

I looked up to the sky and mouthed to my children's father in heaven: *We will be back!*

We headed west. I had to walk on my heels and slowed everyone down.

"Ma, let me carry you," Zhong bent over, waiting for me to climb on his back.

"Let me," Xiao said.

"Don't argue. Let's take turns," Zhong said and waved his hand, signalling the end of the conversation.

The moment I climbed on Zhong's strong solid back, I felt safe, as if the bombs wouldn't fall on us as long as I held onto him.

Then a huge bomb exploded in front of us. The powerful current of hot air knocked us both backwards and we tangled on the ground. Dust and debris blinded my eyes. I shut them tight but couldn't block out the sickly stench of blood mixed with dust and gunpowder. The air was thick and unbearable. Someone shook me. I opened my eyes. My two boys were hovering over me and saying something, but my ears were ringing. They helped me sit up. I shouted to them, "I can't hear you," while checking on my arms and legs. They were all there.

Xiao said something and thrust the green quilt and the bundle of clothes to Zhong and bent over. Zhong helped me climb onto Xiao's back. As we stumbled forward, I saw human skin plastered on a wall. I turned my head away, but limbs, hair, flesh and human entrails were everywhere. I almost threw up.

The panicky throng turned east, carrying us with it. Adults yelled out for their children. Kids cried and the injured moaned. More bombs fell around us. The tide turned south, only to meet head-on with the people running toward us. We were like headless chickens, running blindly and madly. An old woman with bound feet crawled on her hands and knees, ruining her exquisitely embroidered silk clothes.

Xiao tripped over a body and fell. I slipped out of his grasp and landed heavily on the ground again. Zhong took over and pulled me up onto his back. People were dazed and confused. The mass slowed down to a walk.

A young man waved and shouted to us; people followed his direction and turned west, moving faster. Eventually, we made it to the west gate, only to find it jammed like a bottleneck. A few students stood ashore of the current, shouting and gesturing at people, wanting us to form a line, to follow their orders, but no one paid them any attention.

The boys seemed to have formed a plan. Xiao walked in front, elbowing people away. Zhong followed behind him closely with me on his back. We were thrust to the left, then to the right. Finally, we emerged on the other side of the city wall.

Refugees from Kaifeng joined those from the east. I wanted to walk on my own but the boys insisted on taking turns to carry me. They argued that my bound feet would slow us down, and we didn't have a moment to spare. The poisonous sun licked our backs with its flaming tongue. The current of human bodies floated west along the railway tracks. People carried shoulder sacks or pushed loaded carts. When a horse-drawn cart with rubber wheels passed by, it attracted envious glances. They were obviously farmers. Occasionally, we saw someone who rode a donkey or a mule. The city folk had no horse-drawn carts or animals to ride. Men put their young children in baskets and yoked them. Most people were like us, ladened by our belongings, walking on foot. The ringing in my ears had weakened, and I could hear the noise again.

Our land deeds!

"Stop!" I shouted, "Put me down." Zhong put me down and they glared at me.

"I forgot to take our land deeds. We must go back."

"Ma, you must be mad," Zhong said.

"Don't!" Xiao shouted.

"What if our house gets looted? What if a bomb hits it and burns the house down? What proof will we have to claim our properties?" I asked.

"Ma." Zhong was obviously frustrated. "Right now, we should worry about our lives, not the properties. Even if our house burns down, we've been living there for years and everyone knows the land is ours. When we return home, we can always rebuild the house. As the Chinese proverb puts it, as long as the green hills are preserved, there will be no worry of firewood."

"Zhong is right," Xiao said. "Remember how my parents died? Over a sack of grain seeds."

Xiao seemed to have matured overnight. They were right. I had to give up the idea.

When night came, people camped out on the roadside. A heap here and a lump there. Some even slept in the nearby wheat field. Zhong, Xiao and I each had a steamed bun, and then we spread our quilt on the hard ground, just like others around us. The boys soon began to snore, but I couldn't fall asleep. *What if the enemy comes to bomb us in the middle of the night? What if we can't outrun the Japanese troops? Where are my girls right now? Are they also sleeping somewhere in the wilderness? Are they still alive?* After tossing and turning for a long time, I finally drifted into a fitful sleep.

The next morning, bright sunlight woke us. A cuckoo sang: "As they turn yellow, harvest them." At least, that was what my father told me when I was a child. Farmers believed the birds were there to remind them to harvest wheat as fast as they could because no one knew when the rain would come.

This time, I absolutely refused to be carried, and the boys relented. We found a dirty creek and drank from it, sharing the last bun.

"We must find food," Zhong said.

"Let's get a little further," I said. With each minute of delay, the price might be our lives. I thought of my girls again. They were so young. How far could the tender soles of their feet carry them?

Along the way, the flow of refugees became thicker each moment. Holding onto Zhong's elbow, I trudged on. Our faces and shoes were covered with dust. The mass smelled of sweat, unwashed bodies and desperation. And the noises: wheels squeaked, feet stomped, horses and donkeys neighed, children cried, men cursed and the sick coughed and spat. The searing sun was straight above us. The wheat fields along the road had turned golden. The sparrows flew low, pecked off the grain. The sky was blue. A few strands of clouds floated above. How I wished I was a real phoenix and could fly from danger at any moment!

My throat was on fire. "Let's stop. We need to find food and water," I said.

We stopped.

"We still have some money." I looked around and saw a village in the distance. "Let's go there and buy some food."

A low rumbling sound came from above. We looked up and saw black dots in the eastern sky, growing larger by seconds.

"They are here. Run!" a man shouted.

Not again!

The masses exploded before the bombs did. People ran in all directions. Yet I stood there, eyes fixed on the sky, unable to move.

"Run!" Zhong yelled and dragged me to the wheat field. Just as we crouched down, he thrust the quilt over our heads.

Would this be the last moment I lived on earth? Was my husband waiting for me on the other side? Was he watching over us right now? It was summer, yet my teeth chattered. I didn't want to die, not yet, not before I found my daughters.

Boom! Bang! Bang! It was like a recording replayed from the day before. My ears rang. Debris rained down on the quilt. A plane flew so low that the whirlwind almost blew our cover away.

When the sound of planes died down, I stuck my head out from under the quilt. Only then did I realize that the field was golden but the quilt was green. How could it be camouflage? Besides, only Xiao's head was covered, leaving his entire body exposed, like an ostrich burying its head in the sand. But I was in no mood to scold him. People slowly emerged from their hiding places and gathered on the road. A big hole gaped where we had stood. Corpses, limbs and bones were scattered around. People clutched lifeless bodies, howling. Some looked up, cursing at the sky.

A woman wailed beside three corpses, one man and two small children—a boy and a girl. Blood gushed from the wounds on the bodies and stained the soil black. The woman pounded the ground over and over, her knuckles raw and bloody. The passersby averted their eyes. No one helped her. Even I felt numb. I guess when people have too much sorrow of their own, they become numb to others' suffering.

"Let's go," I said to Zhong and Xiao.

"Ma, let us help her bury them," Zhong said, and Xiao nodded like a chicken pecking rice.

Any delay could mean death. But did I want to quench the kindness in my boys' hearts?

"Be quick," I finally said.

Zhong and Xiao squatted beside the woman.

Zhong said, "Let go. We can help you bury them."

The woman ignored him. Blood, tears and snot made her face a sticky mess.

The boys found some shell shards, still burning hot. They wrapped their hands with rags and dug a shallow grave. The woman let go of the corpses. My sons carried and placed the bodies into the hole, the father in the middle, with a child on each side.

I put my arms around the woman. "Sister, you have to live. We must run."

She lifted her face. Her eyes were vacant. "Why should I live when my entire family is dead?"

I didn't know what to say. *If I were her, I wouldn't want to be alive either.* I swallowed hard and let go of her.

She crawled to the grave. I backed up a few steps to give her the space to say her final goodbye. Before anyone realized what she was doing, she picked up a piece of shrapnel and slit her own throat with a swift motion, then collapsed on top of the three bodies inside the grave.

Chapter 13

While my boys buried the family of four, I sat on the ground, unable to move a muscle. The image of that woman slashing her throat played over and over in my mind. Why didn't I see it coming? Had I paid more attention, I might have been able to save her. What happened to her could happen to any of us. If I lost my boys on this journey, what would I do?

We must leave the main road. We must survive.

When Zhong and Xiao gathered around me again, I told them we would go to the nearby village to look for food. They were sombre too, and we hardly talked on the way, only moved our feet mechanically toward the cooking smoke in the distance. By the time we made it to the edge of the village, it was getting dark. Dogs barked intensely. I was sure they smelled desperation in us. Xiao picked up a tree branch, ready to fend them off.

We knocked on the first door at the edge of the village. After a short while, an old man opened it. The moment he saw us, he said, "No food. Go away," and shut the door. We moved to the next door, and the same thing happened. After a third door shut in our faces, it dawned on me that we must look like beggars.

Before the middle-aged man at the fourth home could close his door, I said, "Wait, we are no beggars. We are refugees, and we'll pay you."

He stopped mid-step and looked us up and down.

"We are from Kaifeng, escaping the Japanese. All we want is some food and water," I said.

He opened the door wider and let us in. A family of six, an older couple, a middle-aged woman and two little boys, sat around a stone table in the courtyard, having their supper.

The man said to his family, "They are refugees from Kaifeng."

"Sit down, please." The old man gestured to a few wooden stools nearby.

As we shared a meal of bran cakes and barley gruel with the family, they asked us about our journey.

"Why are you not leaving?" I asked.

"The wheat is ready for harvesting. If we leave now, we will lose it all," the old man said. "Once we harvest the crop, we'll leave with it. At least we'll have food for a year. The problem is, with the war going on, we hardly can get any farmhands this year." He sighed.

"We can help," Zhong said earnestly, looking at me. "Ma, Xiao and I can help with the harvest."

I thought about it. The money we had was not enough for us to make it to safety—wherever that was. Even with money, there were no restaurants or food vendors along the way. The villages, I realized, were safer than the main road.

"Of course you can," I said and turned to the older man. I guessed he was the grandfather and the head of the family. "My boys can work for you. All we need is three meals a day."

The matter was settled.

"How much do I owe you for the supper?" I asked.

"A farmer's meal doesn't cost much," the older man waved his hand.

We stayed in that village for a week, then moved to the next one and offered the same services. Even though we had food and shelter for the time being, I knew we must keep moving as far away from the enemy as we could. Besides, once the harvest was over, no one would hire us and we would have nothing to eat. Village by village, we eventually arrived at Zhengxian, a city smaller than Kaifeng. Many roofs were gone. Ramshackle houses stood with broken beams jutting out from the smoke-blackened walls at odd angles, like broken bones out of flesh. My heart turned cold. I had hoped to find my girls here. Now, I'd rather they had left this place long before the bombing.

We followed the crowd and found the refugee camp in the city. There, men and women were separated into different tents. The camp was set up by the government, and we were provided three meals a day, only soup. At least we had shelter and could fill half of our bellies.

The moment we settled down, we checked out the entire camp in search of my girls but ended up emptyhanded.

"Scour the city tomorrow," I said to the boys.

They didn't find their sisters but brought me news about the Nationalist Army's recruitment posters. They needed male communication officers. The candidates needed to be over age eighteen and pass an exam.

"Ma, I want to give it a try," Zhong said.

"But you told me the deadline had passed," Xiao said.

"The exam date hasn't," Zhong said.

"You want to leave us?" I asked in disbelief. My hands and feet turned cold under the hot summer sun.

Zhong took on a serious tone, "Mother, so many young men have left their mothers to fight the enemies, why not me?"

"But . . ." I wanted to say I *cannot lose you*, but he was right. If all the mothers kept their sons at their side, who would fight the Japanese and defend our country? Defend us?

I changed tactics, "But how do you—"

Zhong cut me off, which almost never happened, "As long as you let me, I'll find a way."

He might not pass the exam, I told myself and reluctantly gave Zhong my consent.

On the morning of the exam date, we all went to the temple where the examination was held. Xiao and I stayed a few yards away, watching Zhong talk with the officer in charge. I couldn't hear what he was saying but I could see him put his palms together and bow repeatedly. Finally, the man said something, and Zhong gave him a very deep bow. Then he turned in our direction and waved.

Zhong was the last one allowed to enter the temple. Xiao and I went back to the camp. By late afternoon, Zhong returned. I asked how he did.

"I feel pretty good," Zhong said. "The first subject was English, my favourite. I knew most of the answers." I didn't even know they taught English in school. How little did I know my son?

Three days later, the names of those who'd passed the exam were posted on a wall in the town centre. A bunch gathered three layers deep in front of the poster. Zhong and Xiao managed to get close. Then Xiao squeezed through the cluster and ran to me.

"Zhong passed! He earned the second highest marks overall!"

I didn't know if I should laugh or cry. Now I wished the boys had never seen that poster, but at the same time, pride rose in my chest. This was the third and last son I was sending to the battlefield. A mother couldn't do more for her country.

Zhong was accepted as a communications officer and scheduled to leave the next day. That night, he said to me, "Ma, I'm sorry I have to leave you this way. You know sometimes it's impossible to be loyal to one's country and to fulfill one's filial duty to one's parents at the same time. Besides, my name means loyalty. Fighting for our country is my duty and destiny."

"I understand." I had learned these lines outside of my brothers' classroom window when I was a child.

Zhong turned to Xiao. "I'm handing over our mother to you in one piece. You must promise me that one day you will return her to me, also in one piece."

"Yes, I promise," Xiao said firmly. He seemed to have grown up overnight.

I had promised my late husband to keep my family together. Now the only person by my side was an adopted son.

Chapter 14

The next morning, the three of us set out from the camp with our bundle and made our way to the train station to bid farewell to Zhong. Once he left, Xiao and I would continue travelling westward. The further we were from the enemy, the safer we would be. Standing on the platform of the train station, I held Zhong's hands and reminded him again to be careful and not to play hero and get shot.

"Ma, you've said this a hundred times." Zhong twisted his body, seeming to want to get away. In his new uniform, he looked sharp and older than his eighteen years. I suddenly realized that he already considered himself an army officer and didn't want to be treated like a child anymore.

"Promise you'll come back," Xiao said and couldn't help but touch Zhong's uniform, hat and belt.

"Don't worry. Once we defeat the Japanese, I'll come home and will never leave you again." Zhong clicked his heels and saluted me and Xiao. I was taken aback and smiled through my tears.

The whistle blasted three times. It was time for us to part. He stepped onto the train.

"Look," Xiao pointed at the head of the train. "Soldiers!" He then pointed at the remaining parts of the train. "Civilians! Maybe we can get on it too."

I followed his finger. Xiao was right.

"But we don't have money to buy tickets," I said.

Xiao nudged my elbow. "Just get on. If we're caught, we will tell them my brother is a soldier and sits in the front. I bet they won't kick us off the train." In the effort of gushing out those words, he flushed terribly.

It made sense. Zhengxian was only a temporary stopping point for the refugees. No one knew when the Japanese would be here. Besides, my girls could be at the next train stop waiting for us. All the bones in my body ached, and my heavy legs could hardly carry me another mile.

I agreed.

Xiao helped me climb onto the train. It was packed. We squeezed through the people blocking the doorway and headed toward the belly of the train. The inside was bigger than I imagined. Even with all the windows open, the stale, hot air filled with the smell of sour sweat, pungent tobacco, dust and dirty shoes. All the old wooden seats were taken, and the overhead racks were stuffed with luggage and bundles. People stood or sat in the aisle, blocking the passage. We picked our way through and eventually found a spot on the floor. Xiao put our bundle down and helped me to sit on it.

With two short and one long whistle, the train began to move. *Good*, I thought. *Once the train leaves the station, we're safe.* I let out a breath, but my stomach growled.

"You look pale," I heard Xiao saying. "I'll find some water."

Moments after Xiao left, a voice called out from one end of the car, "Tickets! Tickets!"

My throat went dry. It was a man in some sort of uniform. I quickly lowered my head, fixing my eyes on the floor, wishing for Xiao to return.

A pair of dirty boots stopped in front of me. I refused to raise my face.

"Ticket!" His voice boomed above me.

I forced myself to lift my eyes and stammered, "I, you see, my son is in the front."

He bent over and glared. "Show me your ticket!"

Heads turned and their gazes were like thorns on my back. My cheeks burnt.

"I don't have one," I blurted out. "My son—"

The man grabbed my collar, lifted me up and dragged me along. I tried to dig in my heels, but it was useless. I felt like a chick being snatched by an owl. The ceiling of the train rushed by above me.

"I beg you, let me go!" I had never been so humiliated. "My son is in the front car—he's in the army!"

He wouldn't answer, wouldn't stop until we were at the door. He opened it with force. No! *Xiao is still on the train! And my children. How will they find me? I can't die like a dog!* I felt a violent push and was airborne. As the wind whizzed past me, all the air was sucked out of my lungs. With a thud, I hit the ground.

"Ma, wake up. Wake up. Oh God, please. Wake up." The voice was faint and far away.

My eyelids were heavy. Now, dying seemed the simplest, easiest way to quit, to get out of this miserable world. Peace—the thing we all wanted so much—was finally near, as long as I refused to open my eyes.

The voice persisted. "Wake up, Ma, wake up, wake up!"

I wanted to say, Go *away*, but no sound came out.

I finally opened my eyes, just to see who was bothering me. At first, I couldn't focus. Only a shadow loomed over me. I blinked a few times until I saw a face, Xiao's face, shiny with sweat and tears.

"Oh, Ma. You're still alive. Thank God! Are you hurt? Can you sit up?"

With one hand holding mine and the other on my back, Xiao helped me to sit up slowly. I tasted salty blood in my mouth. When I spat, a few teeth flew out. I wiggled my toes, and a wave of pain hit me. Xiao rolled up the legs of my pants, revealing blue and purple bruises. My skin was scraped raw and blood trickled down from the open cuts.

Xiao took off his shirt and tore it into pieces before I could stop him.

"What're you doing?" I shouted, but the sound came out of my throat like a whisper.

"Bandaging you up," he said.

"But we have torn clothes in the bundle," I said, not knowing whether to laugh or cry. Anyhow, it was too late. He managed to wrap up my wounded legs.

"How did you find me?" I asked.

When he returned with the water, the other passengers told him what happened. He picked up our bundles and jumped out of the train. "It took me a long time to find you. I called out for you all the way here. I was scared to death," Xiao said. He gathered me in his arms and rocked me slightly.

At this moment, I was like a child and he the adult, my protector and the man I could count on. How *would I survive without him?* I felt loved and secure and didn't want to break out from his embrace. Was this appropriate? So what? We could die tomorrow or the next week.

The war was like a huge pall sheet, wrapping up all the dead and dying. In a way, I was glad that Mr. Ouyang, Rui, my father and my husband had all gone before the war. At least they died in peace and were surrounded by their loved ones. *Are they watching over us right now?* I hoped not, for I had not fulfilled my promise to my husband. Worst of all, I had lost face while being kicked off the train.

Xiao and I sat there for a long time. Then he stood up, put me on his back and walked slowly and doggedly along the train tracks to the west. For a moment, I thought I was on my husband's back. Then I jerked awake. It was not my husband but Xiao!

In the following weeks, Xiao and I knocked on doors, offering labour for food. We had enough scraps to keep us alive. At night, we rested on haystacks or in fields. Even in summer, the weather cooled down during the night and dew often dampened our clothes. In the morning, we would find ourselves snuggled together. Sometimes we were lucky to find a deserted temple and have a roof over our heads.

It normally should have taken about three weeks on foot to get to the next city, but it took us five. When we arrived in Luoyang, tens of thousands of refugees had already gathered there. The refugee camp there was much bigger than the one in Zhengxian. After we settled down, I asked Xiao to go around and see if Daisy and Orchid were there.

They were not.

One day, a man in the soup line, wearing a long, tattered

gown, caught my eye. Only teachers and scholars wore gowns. I got closer to him. "Teacher Guo?"

He turned, blinked behind the thick glasses.

"I'm so glad to see you," I said. "You're Daisy and Orchid's teacher. I'm their mother! I haven't seen them since May twenty-third. Do you know anything about the kids in school?"

"Yes, the Children's Performing Arts Group escaped the town in time, with all the members," Teacher Guo said. He further assured me that the kids must be safe. The group leaders and other teachers were with them.

Thank God! At that moment I wanted to kneel to the Jade Emperor above to express my gratitude.

A few days later, Teacher Guo came to the women's section, waving a newspaper and shouting, "I have good news for you." He unfolded the paper to the second page and read out loud: "The Children's Performing Arts Group of Kaifeng in the flame of war."

My heart leaped to my throat. "Read for me, please."

Teacher Guo cleared his throat. "In May of 1938, the Japanese captured Xiuzhou and continued to encroach west along the Longhai railway route. Kaifeng was threatened from the east, south and north. On May twenty-third, the Education Bureau of Henan province arranged for the Children's Performing Arts Group of Kaifeng to leave the city. The group travelled along the Pinghan railway route, continuing to participate in the anti-Japanese, save-the-country activities. They have left their footprints in many places, including Xuchang, Zhu Ma Dian and Nanyang. They finally arrived in Hankou safely. There, the group produced the musical *The Waif*. The leading role is shared by two eleven-year-old girls, Li Xiulan (Orchid) and Han Caihong (Rainbow). The show was a huge success . . ."

I didn't hear the rest. I snatched the newspaper from his hand and stared at the small square characters, hating myself for not being able to read. Tears dropped on the paper and smudged the ink.

"Do you want to go to Hankou to look for your daughters?" Teacher Guo asked.

"I don't have money for train tickets."

Guo frowned. "In that case, you can send Orchid a telegram to tell her you are here."

"I don't have money to do that either."

"That I can help with," Teacher Guo said.

Chapter 15

Xiao and I stayed in the refugee camp for two months, but we never received a reply from Orchid. Maybe the telegram Mr. Guo sent to her was lost? As long as Buddha was safeguarding my girls, I couldn't ask for more.

The weather grew cold. The government had difficulty maintaining the camp. The soup ration was reduced to once a day, and it was so thin that you could see your own reflection in it. My stomach rumbled all day long and I scanned the ground for crumbs like a hawk searching for prey. When I found one, I stuffed it in my mouth before others could react. If I saw a mouse, I swore I would try to catch it and roast it.

When lifting my head became an effort, I knew we were not far from death. In our separate makeshift huts, we slept all day on the bare straw mattresses and only got up to get our soup. Before the war, beggars in Kaifeng dressed better than we did. I could smell my own sour stench. We hadn't washed since arriving in Luoyang. The disgusting odour in the camp made it hard to breathe. People got sick and died like flies—first the old and young, then men and women in their prime. When a person fell, we just watched for them to die because no one had the strength to help.

People started to talk about going home. Then came the final blow. We were told the government no longer had food to feed us. The refugee camp would be closed in three days.

If I had to die, I wanted to die and be buried at home, next to my husband's shell tomb.

Then we heard airplanes. Not again! Where would we hide? We were in the city with no bushes or fields. In any case, I wasn't strong enough to run. I had done all I could, and now it was up to lao tian ye. As long as all my children were alive, I could let go. But I hadn't heard from my twins since they'd left home more than a year ago and hadn't seen my daughters since they fled Kaifeng. Perhaps I should hold on, just a little longer.

A single airplane flew by, but no bombs fell. Instead, sheets of paper fell from the sky like snowflakes.

After the plane was gone, people slowly emerged from their hiding places and picked up the sheets of paper. We gathered around a man who read a scrap aloud. "Japanese troops have taken control of Kaifeng. The fighting has ceased, and we, the Imperial Army, will assist your newly formed government and you in rebuilding your hometown. You need to live a normal life. Please come home. Your safety is guaranteed."

"Maybe we should go home. If we stay here, we will either starve or freeze to death," someone said.

"Better than being bombed to pieces," a young man retorted.

"The bombing has stopped," an old man argued. "Nobody wants to die far from his hometown."

The young man snapped back, "Do you really believe the

bastards who bombed our city and killed our people?"

I glanced at Xiao. We faced the same dilemma: starve or freeze in winter versus risk being killed by the enemies. But Kaifeng was home. I needed to be there for my children. The apples, dates and persimmons in my well yard would have ripened by now. If I could sell them, I would have a few extra coins for winter clothes and coal.

In the end, we decided to go home. I knew we were gambling with our lives. I could only pray that we had made the right decision.

It was harvest time for corn, sorghum and cotton. We resolved to use the same strategy by offering labour for food. I was so weak that Xiao had to carry me on his back to the first village. Since we had gone through these villages in the summer, the farmers knew us. The first farmer fed us before letting Xiao work. Once we had food in our bellies, we grew stronger each day.

Along the roads, we saw new graves and scattered bones. Corpses had been dug from their shallow graves by wild dogs, and they feasted on the carcasses in broad daylight. Big green-headed flies buzzed around. Crows landed on the bodies and squawked. The air smelled of rotten flesh.

At night, it was so cold that we had to huddle up under the tattered green quilt, gaining warmth from each other. Because of the hard labour, Xiao would fall asleep right away. I often watched his chest rise and fall, watched him turning from a boy to a man in those nights. Was it appropriate for us to be so close physically? But we must survive. Once we got home, I would put distance between us. Fortunately, Xiao was a simple boy. As long as we had food for the day and a place to sleep at night, he was happy.

The number of refugees returning to Kaifeng was a trickle, much thinner than the tide that fled the city a few months ago. Doubt grew like a rolling snowball, bigger and bigger in my mind. Why were so few returning home? Had we made a terrible mistake?

When leaves turned yellow, we saw the outline of Kaifeng, and I sighed with relief—at least it was still there. I was once a proud resident of this ancient city located on the central plain of China, which had been the capital city of several kingdoms, the Bei Song Dynasty being the latest one. Now I was fearful. What kind of fate was ahead? Living under the occupation of an enemy force, what would happen to us?

We arrived at the west gate of the city only to find the gate was locked. On the top of the gate fluttered a Japanese flag which had a white background with a red circle painted in the centre. Japanese called it the Sun Flag. Chinese called it the Plaster Flag because it looked like a Chinese medicine plaster. For me, it was more like a bloody pie flag. The Japanese army called themselves Huangjun—the Imperial Army. I would rather call them the Locust Army, destroying everything in their path.

A few Japanese soldiers patrolled on top of the city wall; rifles slung over their shoulders. Their helmets gleamed under the sun. A poster was pasted on the gate. Someone read it aloud: "To ensure the safety of the residents of Kaifeng, the east, west and north city gates are closed until further notice. The opening hours for the south gate are from six o'clock in the morning to six o'clock in the evening."

A man said, "I bet they just want to ensure their own safety."

Did he mean they were afraid? Were there underground fighters around here?

We walked alongside the city walls, all the way to the south gate. There we were greeted by the corpse of a young man hanging from a pole. He wore no shirt or pants, only boxers. His body was covered with deep red slash wounds, and a white banner with thick black lettering was wrapped around his chest. Having seen so many corpses on the road, I was no longer afraid, only wondering what his crime had been.

I whispered to a young man standing next to us, "What does the banner say?"

"He killed a Japanese soldier," he whispered back.

So he was a fighter. I felt both sad for the young man and excited. When people dared to fight back, we had hope.

The gate was guarded by two Chinese policemen and six Japanese soldiers dressed in uniforms the colour of shit. The Japanese soldiers' helmets had three pieces of fabric resembling pig's ears attached to them, which added to their strange appearance. Two huge wolf-dogs[12] strained on leashes held back by the guards. Their thick, glossy fur was a mix of brown and black. Clearly well-fed, they growled with their tongues hanging out, ears erect and tails hung low like wolves. I saw murder in their eyes.

---

[12] wolf-dog: Chinese name for a German shepherd

A little girl whimpered. The dogs began to bark. The man who held the child covered the girl's face, shushing her. Unwashed and stinky, our skeletal bodies in tattered clothes and dirty shoes made us easy targets. I had no doubt that with one command, those dogs would tear us to pieces. Xiao held my arm with a stiff grip. I knew he, too, was nervous. We didn't dare speak. Maybe we shouldn't have returned after all, but it was too late.

Upon entering the city, we were patted down. People's carts and shoulder sacks were searched as well. After that, we were each given a small Japanese paper flag to write down our name and address and pin the flag to our chest. A Chinese clerk helped the illiterates.

Inside the city wall, debris and ruins lay in the streets. The flame-blackened two-storey building of Sea Dragon Drugstore had new frames installed, but no walls. Broken glass lay scattered on the ground, reflecting the glinting sunlight. So this was what *guo po jia wang* looked like— our country conquered and our family ruined.

We walked along Zhongshan Street. Some houses had new windows. Other mutilated buildings looked like skeletons. Two enemy soldiers guarded the city hall. The gate was open, and I saw Japanese soldiers in training. Xiao and I tiptoed past. To me, they were like the dogs. One false move could cost our lives.

Zhongshan Street lay silent. Only six months ago this road was so crowded that one often had to squeeze by. Now, on both sides of the street, shop after shop was abandoned. Several had changed their name and business. I couldn't read the banners but could see the pictures on display. They were openly selling heroin and opium! A few peddlers wandered about, hoping to sell their goods to fewer pedestrians. Everyone wore the Japanese paper flag.

On the flat asphalt road, fat crows gathered. Their feathers glinted dark blue under the sun, and their beady eyes watched our every move. I had never seen so many of them in the inner city before. Two truckloads of Japanese soldiers sped by. One dragged a cannon behind it. The birds scattered, but soon returned to their turf. They were not afraid of humans at all.

A realization hit me. They must have fed on so much human flesh that they were waiting for us to fall, to die.

When I saw the ridgepoles of my house, my shoulders drooped with relief. It was still standing. I knocked on the door. After a while, it was opened, and Mrs. Lin stood before us.

"My goodness, it's you!" The old woman stared at me as if she saw a ghost.

"Yes, we are back." Suddenly, I lost all the strength in my body and leaned on the door frame.

"Thanks to Buddha that you're alive," Mrs. Lin murmured.

Xiao helped me reach my guest hall and I collapsed on a stool. Mrs. Lin followed us in.

"Ma, you wait here. I will go get some water so we can wash," Xiao said and went out. A moment later he came back, shouting, "Our fruits are gone!"

"What?" I stood up and staggered out.

Mrs. Lin rushed on. "I haven't had a chance to tell you. They were here, and they did this."

"Who did what?" I asked.

"The Japanese soldiers, led by a . . . by your . . . by a man who claimed to be your stepson. They searched the house, found nothing, so they took the fruits."

"Searching for what?"

"They were looking for your sons. They told me to shut up and pushed me aside. After they left, I didn't go to your rooms to check because . . ."

"No need to explain," I said to Mrs. Lin.

The land deeds! I got up and rushed to my bedroom. The clothing trunk was wide open and our clothes were scattered on the floor. Fortunately, the bottom of the trunk was intact. I reached into the secret chamber and fingered around. The documents were still there. I sighed with relief.

The treasure!

"Get me to the storage room," I said to Xiao.

He didn't know anything about the buried treasure. Puzzled, he helped me get to the storage room. The junk was still piled on the floor. Good, our treasure was safe.

At last, we went to the well yard. We had planted four fruit trees there when we first moved into this complex so many years ago. Now, except for a few on high branches, most fruits were gone. What was there for me to sell? Nothing. How were we going to survive the winter? I sat on the ground and bawled, "You dog-fucked Japanese! I'll kill you all!" I had never sworn like this in my entire life.

"Be careful. There might be traitors next door," Mrs. Lin shushed me.

Traitors? I stared at her.

"You don't know?" Mrs. Lin lowered her voice, "In Kaifeng, the Japanese recruited a lot of local ruffians and thugs to work for them. Rumour says they were trained to collect intelligence on our troops. Some even travelled to Zhengxian and Luoyang. They wore our clothes, spoke our language, with no word of traitor written on their faces. You've got to be careful."

Chinese helping the Japanese? What kind of Chinese would do that? Had Qi become a traitor already?

Xiao knelt beside me. "I'll go to Master Chen's restaurant tomorrow. It may still be there, and I may get my old job back."

Mrs. Lin cooked noodles for us that evening. With a full belly, I finally slept in my own bed, in my own house. I should feel good, but I did not. Why were they looking for my sons? What was Qi's role in this whole thing? Would they come again? I stared at the dusty and spiderweb-covered ceiling until the wee hours.

The next morning, we had our few remaining apples and persimmons as breakfast. Then Xiao left home.

By the end of the day, he returned in elation.

"Ma, I got my old job back!"

Chapter 16

The third day after our return, Xiao was at work, and I was cleaning the house when loud clangs on a gong sounded outside. Broom in hand, I went to our front gate, put my ear against it and listened.

"Attention fellow citizens! Those who have not registered for the residential card, go to your local *baozhang*[13] to register. Attention—"

The voice stopped abruptly on the other side of the wooden door.

"Anybody home?" A familiar voice, then someone kicked the door. Startled, I opened it. A man stood facing me, a gong in one hand and a stick in the other.

"Well, well, well! Look at who has come home."

I froze. It was Qi.

---

[13] *Baozhang* was a position in the *baojia* system, which was first invented in the Northern Song Dynasty for the military, but gradually evolved into a social system where the smallest units were households (*hu*) and the household head was called *huzhang*. Ten hu were grouped into a *jia*, which was led by a *jiazhang*; ten jia formed a *bao*, led by a baozhang. The government utilized this system to maintain social order and control at all levels of society with relatively few government officials and police forces. The system was eventually abolished in 1949 when the Communists came into power.

"Don't be so surprised, Mother," Qi said with his typical lopsided smile, but the coldness in his eyes made me shiver.

I tightened my grip on the broom. "What do you want?"

Instead of answering me, he looked around. "Where are my brothers and sisters?"

"They are not here. What do you want?" I repeated my question while sizing him up. The same lanky frame, oily hair parted to one side, and the cleft chin. He wore a black silk shirt and trousers, and a pair of new shoes with thick soles. At his ankles, black strings tied up the loose end of the trousers. I had not seen any refugees who dressed so well and looked so well-fed. Where had his newly found wealth come from?

"Hey, relax. Nobody is going to eat you. Look, I cared for you so much that I've been checking on you. Just returned, huh? I'm here to inform you that all citizens need to register for the new residential card. One cannot move around freely without it." He beat the gong with a loud clang to finish the speech. I almost dropped my broom.

"Where do I get it?"

"You need to go to your baozhang to fill out paperwork and get your identity verified."

"Who is my baozhang?" I asked.

"He's right in front of you." His grin widened. So that was where his wealth came from. He now worked for the Japanese.

"I'll have to wait for Xiao to come home."

"Who is Xiao?"

"My adopted son."

"Wait, you adopted a son? How old is he?"

"He's a big boy."

"Where is he?"

"At work."

"He has found a job so soon?"

I said nothing.

"I don't know if I can verify his identity. Anyhow, you know where to find me."

Qi turned around. I was surprised to see a placard hanging on his back. Four characters were written on it, but I didn't know what they meant. It might be the announcement of his new position.

When Xiao came home, I told him about Qi's visit and the residential card.

"I also heard this from Master Chen," Xiao said. "In Chinese it is called *Liang min zheng*—Good Citizen Certificate. Everyone must have it. The Japanese soldiers search people randomly and beat up those who don't have one. They even throw people in jail for not having it."

After I had two of the steamed buns Xiao brought from the restaurant, we decided to go to Qi's place to get the residential cards. I hated to see him, but there was no way around it.

We arrived at Qi's place. It was the first time I saw this one-courtyard property built by my husband. People in ragged clothes lined up in his yard. Qi sat behind a desk. On it was a stack of paper. We stood at the end of the line. Having more people around us was a good thing.

When it was our turn, Qi took one page from the stack of paper and handed it to me. "Fill out the application and come back with it tomorrow."

When it was Xiao's turn, Qi looked at him and said, "Who are you?"

"I am Li Xiao. This is my mother." Xiao gestured to me.

"She is my mother too. How come I don't know you?"

I stepped forward. "Qi, I told you about him earlier. He's my adopted son."

"Yes, you've told me. But I don't know him. I can't verify his identity. For all I know, he could be one of the fighters against Huangjun."

"Traitor!" Xiao hissed before I could stop him.

"Yes, indeed." Qi walked around from behind the desk and addressed the people in the yard. "I know you guys call me a traitor behind my back. Some, like this little bastard, call me a traitor to my face. If I report him to Huangjun, he'll be dead by tomorrow. I admit I'm a traitor, a hard-core traitor indeed." He turned around and showed the placard on his back to the crowd. "It is written there, a Hard-core Traitor." He faced us again and sputtered, "A hard-core traitor is trusted by Huangjun the most. If I say who is against them, that person will be arrested and perhaps executed. Understand? So your lives are entirely in my hands." His eyes locked with Xiao's.

"Qi, you know he is not against the Japanese." I hated the begging tone in my voice.

"Huangjun. You must address them as Huangjun, not the Japanese. Also, all of you"—he addressed the crowd—"listen. When you are searched on the street, not only do you need to present your residential card immediately, but you also need to bow and say something like, 'Welcome, Huangjun, we support Huangjun.' Better yet, you need to learn how to say, 'We welcome Greater East Asia co-prosperity,' if you want to avoid trouble."

The courtyard was silent. Some stared at him. Some lowered their heads, avoided his glare. I had never seen a person who could be so shameless. But as he'd said, our lives were in his hands.

"Qi, just tell me how can Xiao get a residential card?" I asked.

"Someone who knows him has to verify his identity." Qi sat down behind the desk and crossed his legs.

"I know him," I said.

"A family member doesn't count."

"Ma," Xiao tugged my sleeve. "Let's go home and figure out a way."

We took the forms and went home. On the way, Xiao said he could ask his boss, Master Chen, to verify his identity.

"Hope it will work," I said, and looked at the piece of paper in my hand. "Neither of us knows how to write."

"Ma, why don't you go to the restaurant with me tomorrow? Master Chen can read and write. We may as well ask him to help out with the forms."

The next day, I put a few of the remaining persimmons in a basket and went with Xiao to see Master Chen. The restaurant was rather small, with only six tables, but very clean. When we got there, the door wasn't open yet. We explained why I was there.

Master Chen took the form and glanced at it. "This is very simple. They need to know your name, date of birth, hometown and current home address. A photo is optional."

In a few minutes, he'd completed the form.

"Master Chen, we have another favour to ask," I said. "Can you help verify Xiao's identity for his residential card?"

"Sure. Just tell me what to do."

I told him he needed to go with us to Qi's place to verify that he knew Xiao and that Xiao was a law-abiding citizen.

"After this place is closed today, I'll go with you," Master Chen said.

"Thank you very much." I bowed to him. "I must go now."

"Wait, have you had breakfast?"

I said nothing.

"Why not have breakfast here?" Before I had a chance to say anything, Master Chen said to Xiao, "Go and cook something for your mother."

Xiao disappeared into the kitchen while Master Chen opened the restaurant. Two working men came in. Master Chen took their orders. Xiao came out with a bowl of scalding hot jellied doufu. He put it on the table in front of me. "Have it while it's hot." He ran back to the kitchen.

I held the bowl with both hands. The snow-white bean curds were submerged in broth coloured with dark vinegar, soy sauce, red chili pepper oil and chopped scallions. I inhaled and held my breath. When I let it out, I knew I was in my hometown.

I sliced a piece of bean curd with my spoon, blew on it gently and put it into my mouth. I closed my eyes and stirred it with my tongue. This cheap food, typically for poor people, now tasted like heaven. The silky soft bean curd melted in my mouth before sliding down my throat. I opened my eyes and added two more spoonfuls of chili pepper oil from the tiny cup placed on the table. Spoonful by spoonful, the bean curd mixed with sauce opened a warm path to my stomach, belly, legs and, eventually, the tips of my toes. Life returned to my cold, stiff body. A wave of warmth filled my heart. How could I ever repay Master Chen's kindness?

Two old men entered and called out, "Master Chen, we are here again. How is business?"

"Barely managing." After taking the men's orders, Master Chen disappeared into the kitchen.

The two men had just sat down when a Japanese soldier carrying a rifle walked in. He was about Xiao's age, baby fat still on his cheeks. People stopped talking; all bent their heads over their bowls, busy with their food. The air in the room seemed to stop circulating. My heart skipped a beat. *I don't have a residential card. What if he searches me? What about Xiao?*

"Tea!" he yelled in the direction of the kitchen.

Master Chen rolled out like a meatball. "Huangjun, want tea? Food, too?"

Baby Fat waved his hand. "Food, no. Tea, yes."

Master Chen went away and came back with a kettle and a cup. He poured tea carefully into the cup and set it in front of Baby Fat. Baby Fat blew away the tea leaves gently and sipped carefully while looking around. The two working men paid their bill and fled. One almost tripped over a stool on his way out. I wanted to leave too but didn't dare draw his attention. I lowered my head. The soldier's eyes settled on the two old men. He stood up, holding his teacup, and walked to their table.

"You. Good citizen?" His voice was surprisingly polite.

"Yes, yes, we are good citizens," the two men said and tried to stand up.

"Sit," Baby Fat said, pulled up a stool and sat down at their table. The two men looked at each other, confused and frightened.

Baby Fat smiled, showing two rows of white teeth.

Master Chen sat behind the counter, head buried in a

newspaper. I knew his ears perked up just like mine.

There was silence. Baby Fat was lost for words. He sipped his tea. The two old men ate their food. After an awkward moment, one of them lifted his head and asked, "You, how old?"

"Me?" Baby Fat pointed a thumb to his own chest, "Nineteen."

So . . . he understood some Chinese.

"How old you?" Baby Fat asked.

"I'm sixty-one, and this is my brother, sixty-five," the man said.

"Brother? You brother?" Baby Fat looked back and forth at them.

"Yes, yes," the other man said.

Baby Fat held up three fingers, "I have brother, three."

"Oh," the first man said. "Are they here too?"

"No more," Baby Fat pointed at his uniform. "Soldiers, died. Parents, old, no care." His voice cracked.

The two men looked at each other, obviously not knowing what to say.

"All died." Baby Fat took off his rifle. Everyone froze. Was he going to shoot them? For what? I almost fainted but forced myself to watch. The young soldier used the tip of his bayonet to draw an egg-shaped circle on the dirt floor and wrote two characters in it. He pointed at the writing with the bayonet. "Japan," he said. "Home." Big teardrops fell into the circle, one, two, three. "Go home, no more."

The two men sighed heavily, showing their sympathy.

I stood up and walked quietly to the counter, not wanting to disturb his sorrow.

At the door, I gave Master Chen a slight bow. "How can I thank you?"

"Nonsense." Master Chen bowed back at me. "You are my guest."

"I'll see you later today." I took one last look at Baby Fat, feeling the hate dissipate in my heart.

Chapter 17

Master Chen closed his restaurant early and accompanied us to Qi's home. In my pocket, my right hand held the form tight. By the time we reached Qi's house, the sheet of paper had been dampened by my sweat. The door was wide open. I was glad to see this time fewer people were waiting in line. *It shouldn't take long*, I thought to myself. The three of us went to the end of the line. Qi glanced up at us but said nothing.

When it was our turn, Qi stood up from behind the desk and said, "It's suppertime. Why don't you come back tomorrow?"

I saw Xiao clench his fists without a word. Before I had a chance to say anything, Master Chen took one step forward and smiled at Qi broadly. "Go have your supper. We will wait here."

Qi glared at Master Chen. "Who the heck are you?"

Calm and composed, Master Chen said, "I am Li Xiao's boss, the owner of Peaceful Restaurant. I am here to verify that Li Xiao is my employee and I have known him since—"

Qi waved his hand at Master Chen. "Come back tomorrow."

Master Chen's expression didn't change, as if he didn't

hear what Qi had just said. "Have you heard about my restaurant? A place for coolies, really, but if you don't mind, come to visit us sometime. I'll give you a deep discount." While speaking, he placed his own residential card gingerly on the desk with both hands.

Qi lost his patience. "A place for coolies?" he yelled. "You expect me to eat at your . . . your . . ." Not able to find the right words, he turned to me. "Where is your form?"

I couldn't believe how easily Master Chen handled the situation. Qi scanned our forms and reluctantly issued the cards to Xiao and I, but didn't forget to add, "You know your house is mine, and I *will* take it." His eyes held mine for a brief moment. All I saw was hatred in them.

I said nothing.

We parted from Master Chen outside Qi's door.

On the way home, Xiao asked me if Qi could really take my house away.

"He was bluffing," I said. "If he could, he would already have done that while we were away, right?" As long as I had the land deed, no one could take my house away. Besides, the government also kept a registry of who owned what properties. When property changed hands, the seller and the buyer needed to report the transaction to the government. I had only learned this from Mrs. Lin recently. It was not so easy to just take someone's house away.

We Chinese called the residential card a law-abiding citizen's card because when the Japanese searched us, they always asked, "You, law-abiding citizen?" and we always had to say, "Yes, Huangjun, I am a law-abiding citizen," and some bullshit like, "Welcome, Huangjun. We support Greater East Asia co-prosperity." Those who refused to say such words were often beaten, tied up and dragged away.

Then, out of nowhere, I received a letter from Orchid. With shaking hands, I tore open the envelope and stared at the black square characters. I rushed all the way to Master Chen's restaurant, knowing very well that walking fast on the heels of bound feet was always a spectacle, but I couldn't care less. When Xiao saw me burst through the door, he froze in his tracks with an armful of dishes.

"What happened?"

"News from your sisters. Is Master Chen—?"

As if he heard my voice from the kitchen, the man came out and asked, "What fragrant breeze brought you here?"

Only then did I notice that the customers had stopped eating and were staring at me.

I said to Xiao, "Do your work, and I'll talk to Master Chen." Then, I lowered my voice and asked Master Chen if he could read the letter for me. He ushered me into his kitchen and took the letter. Both Orchid and Daisy had been accepted into the First National High School—a government-sponsored school hidden in the mountains near the west border of Hunan province, over eight hundred li away. It was an area still controlled by the Nationalist government so they were safe. Believing Zhong was still at home, my girls expected a reply from me and asked me to use the address of Fuxing Store in Xixiakou, which would forward the letter, and not to put the name of the school on the envelope or to say anything about the war because letters might be censored by the Japanese. I didn't want to hamper Master Chen from doing business, so I thanked him and left the restaurant.

On my way back home, for the first time in months I noticed how blue the sky was and how light my steps were. Birds chittered happily in the trees, and I couldn't help but smile.

When I got home, I was surprised to see Qi with four Japanese soldiers waiting for me in my courtyard. Mrs. Lin's windows and door were all tightly shut. I felt as if I had been thrown from the ninth cloud all the way to hell.

Qi said, "Mother, we are here on business." He then said something to a Japanese with a small moustache. Moustache yelled out orders. The soldiers stood in front of me, legs apart, with their rifles pointed at me. *Are they going to shoot me? But I didn't break any law.*

"What's your business?" I forced myself to speak in a calm voice.

Qi replied, "My twin brothers have joined the Eighth Route Army, yes? And where's Zhong?"

"No. They just ran away."

"Don't lie to me. They are Communists, and Communists are the enemies of Huangjun. We are here to search your house."

How did he know? Before I had time to think, Moustache shouted, "*Ba ge ya lu!*"

They dashed off in different directions. I heard things being thrown around and broken inside of different rooms, but they came out to the courtyard empty-handed.

"You must report to me when your twins come back. If we find them on our own, you will die with them," Qi barked at me before they left.

I went to my bedroom first, and found my clothing trunk searched again, but the secret chamber remained undiscovered. I then went to the storage room. The same junk was piled there, undisturbed. What was the real reason for the search? I didn't think Qi really believed he would find Wen and Wu in my house. Perhaps he was searching for the property deeds. Or perhaps he'd heard about the buried treasure and was looking for it. Was it possible that my children bragged about it to their friends? Or had Daisy and Orchid told their friends about their brothers joining the Eighth Route Army? They knew about the treasure, and were in the same school with Yu's daughter, Primrose. Yu couldn't keep a secret. Once he knew something, the whole world knew it.

There was a knock on the open door. When I looked up, Mrs. Lin walked in.

"Are you alright?"

"Yes," I said absent-mindedly.

"I'm sorry I opened the door for them. If I refused, they would've brought the whole door down," she said.

"It's not your fault," I said.

"I was too scared to come out."

"No need to explain," I said.

After a moment of silence, Mrs. Lin said, "If they keep coming like this, I don't know how long I can stay here."

I was alarmed. She was my only tenant. If she left, how was I going to put food on the table? Seeing the desperation in my eyes, the woman said hurriedly, "Don't be sad, I'll stay as long as I can."

When Xiao came home, he found me sitting on the edge of my bed, still in a daze. "Ma, are you alright? What happened?" He shook me.

I told him what had happened.

"Bastard!" Xiao spat.

Two weeks later, on a heavy snow day, Qi brought four Japanese to my house again. I recognized Moustache.

"This is a routine search," Qi said. "As long as your family has Communists, we will search your house any time we want."

They ordered Xiao and me to stand in the courtyard, facing the front gate with our heads bowed. After a while, they came out, again empty-handed.

Moustache shouted something to the soldiers. They rushed to Xiao and stripped him naked. The only thing left on his body was the belt of his pants. They pushed and pulled him out of the yard.

"Where are you taking him?" I ran after them. A soldier turned around and smashed my head with the butt of his rifle. As I hit the ground, the sky spun, the earth whirled. Something tasted sticky and salty. Then, nothingness.

I didn't know much time had passed when I heard a voice calling, "Mrs. Li, wake up. Mrs. Li."

A damp cloth was pressed on my forehead. I felt a splitting headache and coughed out something hard. I opened my eyes. Mrs. Lin knelt beside me, wiping off the blood from the corner of my mouth.

"Thank God, you are back. You've lost a few more teeth but you are back."

"Where's Xiao? Where have they taken him?" I looked around.

"They led him away by a leash, like a dog, and made him walk barefoot in the snow."

"I must find him. Help me stand up," I said.

"Perhaps you should drink some water first."

"Get me up!"

Mrs. Lin put her hands under my armpits and tried to pull me up. The sky and the walls spun again. My legs buckled, and I dropped to the ground.

"Let me go and get you some water." Mrs. Lin released me and disappeared into the kitchen. A moment later, she came out holding a squash ladle, lifted my head and fed me some water.

"Do you want me to fetch a doctor?" she asked.

"No. I'll be fine. I need to find Xiao."

At that moment, Xiao walked in, his private parts covered with his hands, his lips purple and teeth chattering. Upon seeing Mrs. Lin, he dashed past us, face flushed crimson like a rooster's comb.

After being beaten and frozen in the cold that day, Xiao fell ill, his body heating up like a smouldering ember. He went back and forth between wakefulness and a dream state, mumbling inaudible words. A few times, he called out, "Golden Dove." Who this person was I did not know. Without money to fetch a doctor, I nursed him with congee and hot ginger tea, and wiped down his feverish body with a damp towel. Whenever his fever subsided and he started to shiver, I wrapped him with a quilt, but his feet were still ice cold. We didn't have any coal left, so I put his feet on my bare bosom to warm them up.

This was how I found a birthmark the size of a coin on his right buttock. When I first saw it, I was transfixed. Something in the bottom of my heart was stirred, but I didn't know what it was. God, what was I doing? Quickly, I covered his midsection. What if someone like Mrs. Lin saw this scene, what would she think of me?

When Mrs. Lin came to visit us, she always brought something: a few eggs here, a package of dry noodles there. One time she brought a pork dish for Xiao. She said he must have good nutritious meals to recover. While Xiao slept, Mrs. Lin told me what the Japanese did to him that day.

"They led him by the leash and paraded the poor boy on the streets while a loudspeaker announced that he was a family member of the Communists. Whenever he didn't walk fast enough, they hit him with the gun stock."

I gasped. Xiao was nineteen years old, a man really. I couldn't imagine how he endured the humiliation.

When Xiao was able to sit at the table and eat a big bowl of noodles, I said to him, "If you want to tell me what happened to you that day, you can."

"I don't want to talk about it." Xiao turned his head away.

I changed the topic.

"Who is Golden Dove?"

"How do you know?" He glanced at me quickly, then looked out to the windows.

"You called out her name in your dream."

"It was horrible. I better not to—"

"Tell me," I demanded.

After a long pause, he said, "There was a banquet in my house. I was married, with a son. I didn't remember his name, but I knew my wife's name: Golden Dove. It was my son's one-month celebration. We had many guests. Then the bandits came. They took our son from my wife's grasp and threw him on the floor, then tried to rape her. She ran straight to the pillar in the guest hall and smashed her head. I charged at the attackers, then a gunshot. I saw myself fall to the ground, lying dead beside my wife and our baby."

Xiao's dream story made the hair on my neck stand up, but I said, "It was only a dream. Perhaps it had something to do with the death of your parents."

"But this is not the first time I have had such a dream. I had it before, just not as complete as this time. I heard when a person has the same dream over and over, it probably was something that happened in his previous life."

"I've heard that too," I said.

Xiao hesitated.

"Go on," I said.

He suddenly knelt in front of me and looked up. Tears streamed down his face. "Ma, I'm afraid I can't be your son anymore."

My heart jumped to my throat. *What? My last son would leave me too?*

"Why?" I cried out.

"I've been looking for my wife, Golden Dove, and . . . and I think I found her."

"Where?" I must be mad too.

Xiao's face turned bright red, but his eyes fixed on me. It was an unfamiliar look that made me nervous.

"Ma . . . Auntie . . . no, Golden Dove, you are my Golden Dove. We were husband and wife in our previous life."

Without thinking, I slapped him, then sank onto a stool, sobbing.

Still kneeling on the floor, he held my legs and cried, "I didn't mean to offend you, but you are really Golden Dove. Don't you remember anything?"

He was mad, truly mad. It must be the fever that tricked

his mind. I calmed down a little and said to him, "Don't ever mention that wife of yours. If you do, I'll . . ." I wanted to say, I *will kick you out*, but truly, after what we had gone through together, I could never do that. He was my son and would always be. I changed mid-sentence, "I'll find you a wife."

From that day on, Xiao didn't mention Golden Dove again but also stopped calling me mother. I knew the whole thing was not over but had no idea what to do. The relationship between us was so taut it was like the string on a Chinese zither. With one stroke of a finger, it could snap.

When I thought things couldn't get worse, Mrs. Lin announced she was moving out.

"With all those horrible things happening, I can't live here anymore. You understand, right?"

What could I say? She had stayed as long as she could. I braced myself for a harder time ahead.

Shortly after Mrs. Lin moved out, Xiao announced that he would move out too.

"But why?" I burst into tears. He had grown on me, become a part of me. If he left, it would be like tearing flesh from my body, and I wouldn't be in one piece anymore.

"Because it's too hard."

I knew what he meant. He wanted to live with me as husband and wife. What should I do? All I knew was I couldn't let him go. I couldn't lose the very last person in my life.

"Why don't you sit down. Let's talk this over," I said.

"Fine." Taking shallow breaths, he looked like a mad bull.

"You agreed to be my son," I started.

"That was then. I didn't know nothing."

"Even if you don't want to be my son anymore, you're still my nephew. Do you really want to leave your poor old aunt?"

"At the most, I'm your adopted nephew." He glowered.

My ears perked up. "What do you mean?"

"The kids in my village said I was adopted. Is it true?"

Now that both his parents were gone, there was no need to hide the truth from him. So I told him, yes, it was true.

"I knew it! I don't share my parents' looks at all."

"That doesn't mean we were once a couple," I sighed.

"Look, my wife's name was Golden Dove. Yours is Golden Phoenix." He talked rapidly, more excited than angry.

"That doesn't mean anything. Golden is very common in Chinese names—Golden Dragon, Golden Phoenix, Golden Lock, Golden Bell."

"It's a hint. God left us a hint, and you have moved up from a dove to a phoenix."

I couldn't help but laugh. How could I make this poor, mad boy normal again?

"And I have a birthmark. Maybe this will remind you of something." Xiao proceeded to pull down his trousers.

"Don't!" I shouted. "How can a birthmark prove anything?"

His hands froze, and he blushed. After an awkward moment, he said, "If you don't believe me, let's go find a high monk who has obtained heaven's eyes. They can see into people's previous lives."

"But we don't have anything for the temple," I said.

"I forgot to tell you the good news. By the end of the

month, I'll finish my apprenticeship and will get paid a weekly wage. We'll have money to buy joss sticks for the temple."

I agreed, only to prove that he was wrong and to put his wild idea out of his mind once and for all.

Chapter 18

When Xiao received his first pay, we spent a good portion on incense. Not every monk has heaven's eyes. We needed a high monk.

When I saw the huge trees in the yard at Xiangguo Temple, I felt both comforted and sad. This was where I had participated in my only beauty contest, at age nineteen, and where my late husband met Mr. Ouyang. That carefree time seemed as if it was only yesterday. I once had a husband and a full house of children. In a blink of an eye, Xiao was the only one who remained by my side. The temple was quite empty now, so we didn't need to wait in line. This was the first time I was about to see a high monk, and I was a little nervous. After telling a serving monk of our purpose, he led us to a side room off the main hall.

A very old monk sat on a cushion. Behind him was a golden statue of a Buddha, much smaller than the one in the main hall. Joss sticks burned, and the room was filled with the scent. Xiao and I ketoued to the Buddha, lit the incense and came to kneel on the cushions in front of the monk.

"What is your *sheng chen ba zi*[14]?"

There was a problem. I knew the time and date of my

birth, but Xiao knew only the date of his birth, not the time.

We told the monk about Xiao's problem. He said he would try his best. He closed his eyes and mumbled some chant. I was sure this was to help him to open his heaven's eyes. After a long while, his earthly eyes opened again.

"What I saw was that you were once a couple, living in the countryside. You had a baby, but your lives were cut short by a terrible event. There were gunshots, blood everywhere."

I couldn't believe my ears.

"But, *Shifu*," I said, "allow me to ask. Usually, when people die at the same time, they reincarnate in the same year, right?"

"In your case, he was delayed three days in the other world. That equals twenty-seven years on earth."

We thanked the monk and came out of the room. I was dazed, but Xiao was ecstatic.

When we got home, Xiao's next request was as shocking as our new discovery.

"Golden Dove, I vowed to find you and spend another lifetime with you. Now I have. Please be my wife again."

"Are you mad? I'm twenty-seven years older than you! I don't even have all my teeth."

"Age on earth means nothing to me. Can't you see? Our lives were cut short in our previous lives, but God gives us another chance. You've suffered so much. All I want to do is to look after you."

---

14 *sheng chen ba zi*: the date and time of one's birth according to the lunar calendar.

I blinked away my tears. *If I truly love this man, I must resist.* "I'm too old for you. I can never give you any children."

"All I need is you. I can have children in my next life."

What will the neighbours say? How can I tell my children? No one would believe this wild story of ours. Moreover, in this world, an old husband with a young wife was common, but not the other way around.

"People will say I used witchcraft and seduced you," I said.

"Let's have a secret wedding then. We don't have to tell anyone."

"What took you so long? Had we been born in the same year . . ."

"It must have taken me three days to find you. I had to know where you landed, right?"

I chuckled through my tears. He made it sound like we'd parachuted to earth, but I still wouldn't accept his marriage proposal.

"In that case, I'll go back to that high monk and ask for his help."

"You can't do that! You will get both of us exposed." I didn't want to be seen as a sinful woman in others' eyes.

We argued every day. He was a man, not a boy, and definitely not my son. I couldn't help but notice his wide shoulders, big chest and bulging biceps. I hadn't had sex since my husband passed away. I longed for a shoulder to cry on, for strong arms to hold me, to make me feel safe. I missed the intimacy between a man and a woman. If I were selfish, I would have said yes right away. But I couldn't do that to Xiao. He deserved a family, not an old woman. Besides, I would die first. Then he would be left alone in this world.

At the end of two weeks, we both were tired of arguing. One day, as I was kneading a piece of dough in the kitchen, Xiao approached me from behind and held me, kissed my neck. My hands were covered with wheat flour. Shocked to dumbness, I just stood there with my arms in the air, letting him spin me around. He kissed my lips with hot breath. Where was that timid boy who would blush before speaking, who would always follow my lead and do what he was told? As his heart drummed against my chest, his tongue tasted like fire. Holding me with one hand, his other hand reached under my shirt and cupped one of my breasts. I collapsed into his arms as if I had no bones in my body. I didn't know I had longed for a man's touch for so long. All my resolve was dissolved at that moment.

We made it to the bedroom. Afterwards, we lay side by side in the dark.

"Fine. Let's get married, with one condition: we must keep our relationship a secret," I said.

"Golden Dove. I'll only call you Golden Dove," he murmured.

"But in public, you may call me Auntie," I said.

For our wedding, at the very least we should wear new clothes and new shoes. Also, my old quilts were tattered; we needed new quilts and pillows. The bottom line was we needed money to live, and Xiao's meagre wages weren't enough. He couldn't even afford a ring. I had to sell something.

First, I thought of the treasure, but once I put it on the market, Qi would know and would lead the Japanese to my house and take the rest away. I couldn't let that happen. I couldn't sell a part of my house either because I had promised my late husband never to do that. After the war, all my children would come home, get married and have families of their own. This house was my husband's provision.

Then I remembered the ten mu of reed marshland that my husband bought years ago. On his deathbed, he told me I could sell it when the value went up. I had no idea if the value had gone up or down. I needed help. The only person I could think of was Master Chen. I took out all the land deeds, put them carefully in the inner pocket of my cotton-padded winter jacket and went to see him.

Master Chen picked out the deed of the marshland. I asked him to find a buyer for me. He told me he would try, but he doubted anyone would want to buy land during wartime, especially marshland.

"If I have to, I'll lower the price until there is a buyer," I said.

By offering a deep discount, I finally found an interested buyer. He put down a deposit. Once he surveyed the land, he would pay me the rest, and the deed would be transferred to his name. It was arranged that the four of us, Xiao, Master Chen, the buyer and I would go together to the marshland the next day.

The buyer rented two rickshaws for us. Xiao and I were in one, and Master Chen and the buyer were in the other. We left by the south city gate. A truckload of Japanese soldiers sped by, guns in hands and helmets shining. By the time we arrived at the marshland, we saw the truck, and the Japanese were there too. What was going on? The rickshaw pullers refused to get close, so we stopped at a safe distance, watching. A Japanese soldier was pushed off the truck, hands tight behind his back. He was dragged into the reeds, facing away. The mud was waist-high. They let go of him; he struggled to walk further into the marsh. Then, bang, bang! They shot him in the back, and he fell into the water like a stone.

Had I just witnessed the Japanese killing one of their own? But why? Baby Fat's face flashed through my mind. I hoped it was not him.

"Let's go back!" the buyer shouted.

I knew the deal was off.

In the end, I had to pawn the ten-mu marshland to a pawn shop. They typically paid only half of the item's worth and, therefore, it was the last resort people would take. Even though I could take the item back within the redemption period, I didn't think I could raise enough money. Xiao was there to put his fingerprint onto the bill of sale, because as a woman, I had no right to sell properties.

Using the money, I bought fabric, multi-coloured silk threads for making new clothes, shoes and bed linens. I tried to spend as little as possible. For our quilt, instead of buying new cotton, I peeled off the old covers and took the stuffing to a cotton fluffer. Afterwards, it was almost as good as new. I couldn't afford silk or satin for wedding clothes either, so I made cotton clothes. I could afford red paper, though. When people got married, a red paper cut-out of the words "double happiness" (interlocking the two words into one) would be pasted on the walls, doors and windows. Since our wedding was a secret, and it would remain that way, I only cut out birds and flowers and put them on our paper-covered latticed windows.

Normally a dragon and a phoenix were embroidered on a wedding quilt, but that would cost too much in silk thread. Instead, I embroidered birds and plum blossoms on our new quilt and pillows.

After all this spending, I still had some money left for a sack of wheat flour, cooking oil, coal and kerosene for lamps. I hid the rest of the money in the secret compartment in our clothing trunk with the land deeds, planning to buy a few chicks in the spring so one day we would have eggs.

We chose the Spring Festival as our wedding day. Xiao got three days off. He bought pork and Chinese cabbage for making dumplings, and some wine.

The wedding was held in our reception hall. There were only two of us. We burnt joss sticks for our ancestors, ketoued to heaven and earth, then bowed to each other.

That night, I was drunk and happy.

Chapter 19

In my entire life, happiness always seemed short-lived, and the nightmares never seemed to end. The day after our wedding, Qi led the Japanese to search my house again. When they found nothing, they ordered us to kneel in the courtyard. A pair of boots stopped in front of me. The cold steel tip of a bayonet pointed at my heart.

"Where are my brothers? This is your last chance!" Qi shouted.

"I don't know," I said in a whisper.

A Huangjun said something to Qi, and he translated, "Open your mouth!"

I knew if I refused, I probably would be killed on the spot. I had seen Chinese killed for no reason at all. I closed my eyes and opened my mouth, not knowing what was going to happen next.

I heard the unzipping of pants, and a stream of smelly urine shot into my mouth. I tried to close it.

Qi shouted, "Swallow or die!"

I burst into tears, closing my fists so tight that my fingernails dug into my palms. *Bastards! The sons of bitches! Dog-fucked!* I wanted to gouge out their eyes, peel off their skins and draw out their tendons with my bare hands. The pungent, salty, bitter stream stung my eyes and flooded my throat. Hating myself for being such a coward, I swallowed my shame. I had never felt so helpless. *Zhong, Wen, Wu, where are you? Kill them all! Burn them all!*

When the flow stopped, I was delirious and crumpled into a pathetic heap on the ground. Just when I thought I had experienced the most unspeakable horror and humiliation, I was picked up by the collar into a kneeling position again. Moustache stepped forward and pried my mouth open with his hands. *Not again!* I once more closed my eyes, only to feel something big and meaty jabbed into my mouth. It was his penis! I realized what he wanted me to do. He held my head with both hands, pushed and pulled. I coughed and gagged, then threw up. He enjoyed himself in my vomit and came into my mouth.

The moment they left our courtyard, I threw up violently, until there was nothing left in my stomach. How could I allow this to happen? Why didn't I bite off his penis? What kind of woman had I become in the eyes of my new husband? I must die. So many Chinese women killed themselves to avoid being raped or afterwards. Why should I treasure my life so much? I didn't deserve to be alive because I was forever tarnished and could never make myself clean again.

I ran into my room, found a rope and tried to make a death loop. My hands shook so much that I couldn't make it work.

Xiao rushed in from the yard and held me back. "Don't do this. I need you. Your children need you."

I tried to get away from his grasp. He cried out, "If you die, Qi will get this house. Is that what you want?"

I stopped struggling, wept soundlessly. He was right. I couldn't let Qi get what he wanted. I must be here waiting for my children. I also wanted to see the Japanese defeated one day.

When my tears dried, I got up, washed my mouth and my face clean, and made two decisions. I would fight back and I would never let Xiao kiss my mouth again.

The next day, I paid a visit to a contact person with the underground network. We had met once before when I arranged for the twins' departure. He was an old man living in the other part of the city. I didn't even know his name. He was known as Number 308.

I knocked on his door using the code from a year ago, three light taps and three heavy ones, hoping it would work. Number 308 opened the door. When he saw me, he quickly looked down both directions of the street, ushered me in and closed the door behind us.

After we sat in his living room, he asked, "How are you doing?"

"I'm still alive." I smiled sadly. He nodded.

"Listen, I want to do something for the Communists. Anything." I wasn't in the mood for small talk.

"That's great." He thought for a moment. "Can you sew?"

"Of course. I used to be a seamstress," I said.

"Our soldiers need clothes, especially cotton-padded winter jackets. You must do it at night, with your windows covered. If you are found out by either the traitors or the Japanese . . ." He trailed off.

"I have suffered worse than death. I'm no longer afraid," I said.

He looked at me curiously, as though he wanted to ask something, but stopped. "You will be Number 309 from now on. Nobody within the network should know your real name. You must always remember that."

"Yes."

"Unfortunately, the network doesn't have money to buy you materials."

"Don't worry, I have some money," I said. *Forget about buying chicks this spring.*

"When you finish a jacket, come to me, and I will tell you where and how to deliver it. You mustn't tell anyone."

"Of course not," I said.

I later learned that, unlike the Nationalist Army, the Communist army was ill-equipped. They didn't have enough financial resources so they relied on a massive network of ordinary people to make clothes for their soldiers. I'd had plenty of experience working behind covered windows at night when I was living in my in-laws' house.

From that day on, each night after the city went to sleep, I went to work. Instead of covering my windows, I draped a thick cotton quilt over the dining table, lit a tiny oil lamp, and sewed under the table. I often wondered if one of the jackets I made would end up on my son's back. When I was too tired to continue, I would tell myself this one is for my son, and keep going.

When I finished my first winter jacket, I was instructed to wear it under my own clothes and deliver it to Number 310's house, in a village outside the city. After that, on average, I delivered one jacket a week. Wearing only a two-layered jacket, I often froze on the way back. Every time I passed the city gate, I needed to present my residential card, and was thoroughly searched.

In the spring, I made shirts and trousers, and delivered a few pieces each trip.

By the summer of 1939, I had been making clothes for the Eighth Route Army for a few months. One day, when I returned from another delivery, Number 308 sat me down. "You're the most productive member of Kaifeng's underground network. The party is very pleased. I wonder if you would be willing to take on more work."

"Just tell me."

"We need messengers. Can you do it?"

"Yes." I was so excited. It felt like I was fighting alongside my twins.

I was taught to hide the tiny pieces of paper in my bamboo cane and deliver them to Number 310. If the message was discovered by the Japanese or by a traitor, I would be arrested, probably tortured or killed. But ever since that day in my courtyard, I was no longer afraid of death. I did this not only for China; I did it for myself, for Xiao and for my family.

I hadn't heard any news from Wen since I said goodbye to the twins four years earlier. Finally, I received a letter from him through the network. Number 308 read it for me. Wen had been trained by the Bethune Medical School in Shanbei[15] and had become a paramedic. He had wanted to be a doctor since he was a child when a surgeon removed a benign tumour from one of his armpits. At the

---

[15] Shanbei: Northern Shaanxi, the territory occupied by the Communists

time, very few Chinese doctors practised Western medicine, and even fewer patients had gone through surgery. It was such a wonder to him. I was so glad that he was realizing his dream.

I also learned that Wu had become a foot soldier. I was worried about them, especially Wu. That boy was brave but not very clever. I pressed the letter against my cheek, didn't want to let it go. But in the end, I knew I had to burn it.

I had not heard from Zhong since he enlisted as a communications officer for the Nationalists in Luoyang. We lived in enemy-occupied territory, and the Nationalists didn't have a massive underground network. I guessed that was why Zhong couldn't write to me. I missed my daughters terribly too, but at least I knew where they were and that they were safe.

Chapter 20

Two and half years after the Japanese occupied Kaifeng, Daisy appeared at my doorstep. At age fifteen, she was taller but pale and thin, and looked exhausted.

I had dreamt of this moment for a long time, yet when she stood in front of me, I didn't know whether I should laugh or cry. All she said was, "Ma . . ." and collapsed.

Xiao and I helped her into the house. After she drank some hot water and ate a cornmeal bun, I asked how she had travelled eight hundred li to get here.

Leaning on a pile of pillows, Daisy fought to keep her eyes open. "Training Officer Jing bought a train ticket for me." When Jing, their school training officer, accidentally blew his own fingers off with his gun, Daisy and others accompanied him to the hospital in Laohekou. When Officer Jing was ready to return to school, Daisy told him she wanted to go home. She told him that she was ill, and didn't want to die without seeing me. Officer Jing paid for her train ticket. Her health problem was heavy menstrual flow and painful cramps.

My silly girl. She had no idea what she had done to herself. Coming into the city was easy, but once you registered as a resident of Kaifeng, it was hard to leave. But how could I scold her for being afraid of dying and wanting to see me one last time?

We just had to make the best of the situation.

I also faced another problem. What would I do about Xiao? I certainly couldn't tell Daisy that Xiao and I were married.

I had to send Xiao back to his own room to sleep.

I also had to report Daisy's return to Qi and apply for a residential card for her. This card was her shackles. She would be forever locked in this hellish city.

Over the following days, I learned bits and pieces about life at the First National High School. The Nationalist government paid their tuition and provided food and shelter. They had great teachers too. Most of the students were separated from their parents during the escape from the Japanese. Some of them were war orphans. The semi-military life was hard for Daisy, but Orchid seemed to thrive. I was so glad that God had kept my youngest daughter from harm's way.

I cooked for Daisy and wouldn't let her get out of bed. I didn't know what was wrong with her and had to ask Xiao to fetch Dr. Cui.

It turned out that Daisy's menstrual bleeding was of no consequence. After taking the Chinese herbs prescribed by the doctor for a month, Daisy's symptoms disappeared.

Disobeying me, Xiao often snuck into my room during the night and left before dawn. I didn't know how much longer we could keep it from Daisy. But it was a small worry compared with my biggest fear. What if Qi and the Japanese came again? Daisy was still a virgin. If she had to suffer what I . . . I didn't dare to continue my thought.

But come they did.

One morning, Xiao left home but returned in minutes. "Qi and the Japanese are heading here. What do we do?"

"Daisy, go hide in the attic in the Phoenix Courtyard. Quick!" I barked.

Just as Daisy disappeared into the other courtyard, Qi led a group of Japanese in.

"We need another search. Your daughter may have brought a Communist lover home, or your twins may have returned as well," Qi said with a cold smile.

I said nothing. I had no words for this animal.

When they headed to the Phoenix Courtyard, I stopped breathing. As usual, Xiao and I were ordered to stay in the main courtyard, not to talk or walk around. *Please, Lao Tian Ye, don't let them find her. I beg you. If you can save her, I will bring you a big offering. Please, please, please!* I heard a door being kicked open, then a man yelling and Daisy crying. I ran to her like a wild animal.

Just as I crossed the threshold of the two-storey building, my daughter was rolling down the stairs like a crumpled paper ball. A Japanese soldier stood at the top of the stairs, watching. I knelt beside Daisy and gathered her in my arms. The soldier came down and walked past us nonchalantly, and they left.

Xiao rushed in.

"Are you hurt? Can you move?" I asked urgently.

Daisy's eyes were shut. She moaned, and tears seeped out from the corners of her eyes.

"It hurts." Her voice was barely audible.

"Where?"

"My back."

I rolled up her shirt. She was all purple and blue, and her lower back was badly bruised.

"What happened?" Xiao asked.

"He found me, beat me with the butt of his gun and kicked me down the stairs. My ribs may be broken. I can't move."

Xiao and I managed to carry Daisy to bed. I asked Xiao to get Dr. Cui quickly.

As we feared, Daisy had two broken ribs. As Dr. Cui felt Daisy's lower back through her underclothes, he said, "She has an injury here. A lump is forming. Keep a close eye on it. I can set her bones, but I'm afraid I can't make the lump go away."

Dr. Cui set the bones for Daisy and tied two pieces of plywood around her torso to keep her still. Daisy screamed throughout. The doctor then took out a small package from his medicine box and handed it to me. "This is the white powder from Yunnan. Give it to her three times a day to help with the pain. Also, make sure she takes deep breaths or coughs every hour or so to prevent pneumonia. It will be painful, but it's extremely important. I'll be back in three days."

Within days, the lump in Daisy's back grew as big as an orange.

Dr. Cui came back every few days. After three months, Daisy's ribs healed. She was able to walk but couldn't stand up straight. The lump didn't go away, either. Dr. Cui said this was the best he could do.

Daisy stooped like an old woman. I didn't know how to comfort her or get her out of her misery. Then one day, Daisy sat me down and said to me, "Ma, I hate the Japanese. I must do something. Otherwise, I will go mad."

How could I have forgotten that working is the best medicine to cure unhappiness? Daisy soon found a temporary office job with an underground organization called Three Principles Youth League—an anti-Japanese youth organization newly established by the Nationalists. Daisy's job was to clean the office, make tea and arrange the tables and chairs before meetings. The money was meagre, and the work was tedious, but she was happy.

How I wished my daughter had never come home.

Chapter 21

In the summer of 1941, Wu sent a note through the underground network. Injured and hidden in a nearby village, my son needed food, medicine and bandages. How badly was he hurt? What was going on? Why was he not with his infantry unit? All these questions swirled in my mind while I prepared for the visit—the first one since the twins left home. Four years of separation, and now I was about to see him. I didn't know if it was a good thing or bad. Returning to enemy-occupied Kaifeng was like jumping into a wolves' cave. Daisy's fate had proven it. I had wanted my children to return home, but not now. I bought the medicine and bandages from the Sea Dragon Drugstore, made ten steamed buns and tucked some cash in my inner pocket, then hurried to the village.

I found Wu in a peasant's house. He wore civilian clothes. His bandaged left arm hung from a sling, and dark circles rimmed his bloodshot eyes. When he left home, he was a slim sixteen-year-old boy. Now, at age twenty, he was as strong as an oak tree. The villager, a Communist sympathizer, went to the front gate to watch out for us.

I held my son's hands. "Why are you here?" I blurted out.

"Ma, I'm so glad to see you. I had no choice. Please sit down, and I'll tell you everything."

This was Wu's story.

About a week earlier, his platoon was on a mission and became separated from the main company. The platoon encountered Japanese bombers. When a bomb exploded near Wu, a piece of shell hit him and he lost consciousness. When he woke up, he had a big gash on his left arm and couldn't hear a thing. He climbed out of the crater and found all his comrades dead. He had no food, no medicine and no way to find the main company. He tore up his shirt, bandaged himself, tore off the red badges on his uniform, threw away his weapon and travelled here as a civilian. Fortunately, he had regained his hearing.

"How have you survived?" I asked.

"On wild plants and roots. I pretended to be a workman returning home when passing through villages. When I asked for water, they often gave me food too."

I told Wu what Qi had done to our family and why I couldn't take him home. I skipped some details, for a mother could never tell a son about her rape.

Wu exploded. "That bastard traitor! I'll kill him."

I left some cash and the supplies with Wu and returned home.

A week later, when I visited Wu again, he was panicky. The baozhang in the village had questioned the host about Wu. The local baozhang oversaw the security of his neighbourhood and was not someone to be taken lightly. The host claimed Wu was a relative, but the baozhang didn't believe him and threatened to report him to the Japanese.

This scared me to death. We had to work out a plan.

The host said this man was unpredictable, but he had one weakness: money. I asked the host to point out the baozhang's house and went straight to him. I begged him not to report my son and gave him all the money I had with me.

I knew I couldn't keep the baozhang's mouth shut forever. I had to move my son elsewhere. I returned home and discussed the issue with Daisy and Xiao. Xiao said he would ask Master Chen for help.

"What makes you think your boss would do that?" I asked. "If anyone found out he was harbouring a Communist, he may lose his life."

"Master Chen hates the Japanese's guts."

Xiao told us his boss' story.

He grew up in a village in Henan, then came to Kaifeng to make a better living, working as a cook in a restaurant for ten years before opening his own. The rest of his family still lived in the countryside. To hide from the Japanese, they dug a tunnel in their courtyard. It had two entrances: one in the courtyard and the other behind the house, outside the back wall. Every time the Japanese came to the village, the whole family would get in the tunnel from the courtyard. The youngest boy—the most athletic one in the family—always remained outside to cover the entrance with straw and other junk. He then would jump over the back wall and enter the tunnel from the other entrance.

They escaped the Japanese that way many times, until the last time.

When the Japanese charged into the village, the entire family got into the tunnel as usual, and the younger brother remained outside to cover the entrance. The family waited for a long time for him to show up, but he never did.

Eventually, when the noises outside died down, the family cautiously crawled out of the tunnel. Before their eyes was the boy's corpse tied to a tree. His chest and stomach were slashed open and his entrails scattered everywhere.

When Xiao finished, I said, "Ask Master Chen for the favour."

Xiao was right—Master Chen agreed without hesitation. Copying his family's strategy, he also had a tunnel in his courtyard. He offered to hide Wu in his house. When there was danger, Wu could get into the tunnel at a moment's notice.

The next challenge was how to smuggle Wu into the city. He didn't have a residential card, and the Japanese had set up checkpoints at every city gate.

I approached the Underground Communists' Network through Number 308. A meeting was arranged between me and the man in charge. I told him my son's story.

"Don't worry. We will do all we can to help him," he said.

Three days later, we met in a different location, and he told me the plan.

The Japanese in Kaifeng needed food and hay from the surrounding villages for their soldiers and horses. They called it a tax. The puppet government ordered each village to take turns providing the supplies. The next scheduled hay delivery time was four days away. The leader had arranged for a group of underground network members from the countryside to take over the job and hide Wu in the hay in a horse-drawn cart. Once the cart was inside the city, they would unload Wu before sending the hay to the Japanese.

"There is one risk, though," he cautioned me. "At the checkpoint, the Japanese soldiers may poke the hay with their bayonets, just to make sure there's nothing hidden in it."

I gasped. *What if they find Wu?*

The leader seemed to have read my mind. "We will wrap him up with thick clothes and hide a dead cat with fresh stab wounds in the hay, in case the bayonet injures Wu, and they find his blood on it. As long as Wu doesn't cry out, one of us will pull out the dead cat to cover it up."

It was a very risky plan. So many things could go wrong. What if the bayonet stabbed him too deep and he cried out or was killed? What if the Japanese didn't believe the cat story and insisted on searching the hay?

"So he is going to take a chance with his life?" I said.

"True. Do you have a better plan?"

I hated to admit I didn't.

"Even after he's been smuggled in, he doesn't have a residential card. Does this mean he can never leave his hidden place, like a prisoner?" I asked.

"Let's worry about that later," the leader said.

"Is there anything I can do to help?"

"Stay home and wait for the news."

I hardly slept that night. When I drifted into sleep the next morning, I dreamt Wu was stabbed and captured. I tried to run to him, but my legs wouldn't move. I must have screamed because Xiao woke me up. I opened my eyes, and it took me a while to realize I was lying in bed, in my home, Xiao beside me. What a relief! Then it dawned on me that Wu was not out of danger yet.

Chapter 22

On the day Wu was supposed to be smuggled into the city, I couldn't sit still and paced in my courtyard all day long. I was not allowed to be near the city gate where the horse-drawn cart was supposed to enter.

Just as dusk fell, Xiao came home from the restaurant with a big smile on his face. "Golden Dove," he said, "it worked! He's safe!"

A Japanese soldier indeed poked the hay with his bayonet. The tip of it stopped just inches away from Wu's neck. Had Wu not been a disciplined soldier, he might have panicked and given himself away.

Wu was unloaded and delivered to Master Chen's house. From that day, he began his hidden life in Kaifeng. Wu reported his whereabouts to his superior in Yan'an through the underground network and waited for assignment. The initial reply was to wait. When the second order came, Wu had completely recovered from his injury. He was assigned a job as a messenger for the underground network, the same job that I was doing. I chuckled. Hiding in Master Chen's tunnel, Wu was literally *underground*.

Even though my son and I lived in the same city, we were not allowed to meet. I went to Number 308 and asked why we were not allowed to work together.

"Because Qi may follow you and discover Wu," Number 308 said.

"Why not get Qi killed, then?" The moment the words escaped my lips, I was stunned. Did I really want my late husband's son dead? Did I hate him that much?

"This type of job is done by professional spies and assassins, not us." Number 308 said.

"Don't we have professional spies and assassins?" I asked.

"Of course we do. All the messages you send out, where do you think they come from?"

"But traitors like Qi endanger our missions and our men; why not get rid of them?" I supposed I indeed hated Qi that much.

"I don't know. I only take orders. Living in the same city, I bet sooner or later you two will bump into each other."

The opportunity came sooner than I expected. Hardly two weeks passed and Number 308 came to my house to inform me that Wu needed to regularly carry intelligence to the upstream bank of the Yellow River, to another member. The message would then be coded and transmitted to Yan'an. For the first meeting, Wu needed not only a secret password, but also his party membership card.

"But having the card on him would be too dangerous," said Number 308. "If he is caught, he would be discovered instantly. Another person should carry his membership card and meet him and his contact at the predetermined place."

"You want me to do it?" I asked.

"It's not my order. It's from the network. The trip is not

long, but . . ." Number 308 glanced at my bound feet and trailed off.

"I can do it. It's just that . . . not long ago you told me my son and I are not allowed to work together. What made the organization change its mind?"

"Because," Number 308 paused and looked me deep in the eyes, "a mother would never betray a son."

The night before our mission day, I sewed Wu's party membership card inside my cotton-padded jacket, along the bottom edge where I could feel it and easily cut the stitches to get it out. I was glad it was winter; the thick winter jacket hid the card. Snow fell like goose down. Holding a bamboo cane and wrapping my head with a thick scarf, I set off upstream of Yellow River.

I passed the north city gate without a hitch. By now, I had gone through the city gates so many times that the checkpoints no longer scared me. I hadn't felt so purposeful, so alive for a long time. I had suffered for too long. It was the time to fight back, side by side with my son. Number 308 was right. I would rather die than betray my son.

The walking distance between Kaifeng and my destination, Zhang Clan village, was about an hour and a half, that is, for a normal person. With bound feet, however, it took me the entire morning. The blacksmith's workshop was easy to spot as it was the only one in the village. When I stepped over the doorsill of the inner courtyard, I tripped and almost fell. The blacksmith grabbed my arm and steadied me. Was this an omen of bad luck? I brushed the thought away.

The room was rather warm. Upon seeing me, Wu stepped forward to hold my hands.

"Ma, you are finally here. We've been worried about you, in this weather . . ."

A stranger also stood up. "I have heard everything about you. Thank you for doing this for us."

"This is Comrade Zhang, my contact," Wu said. "I hope there was no trouble on your way here. Have you noticed anyone following you?"

"No," I said. "I have been doing this for a while, and I know how to get rid of a tail."

I cut the stitches and took out Wu's party membership card. Comrade Zhang examined it and handed it back to me. Using the needle and thread I'd brought with me, I re-stitched the card back in my jacket.

"Have lunch here before you go home," the blacksmith said.

"We have to travel separately," Wu said. "I'm not hungry, and I have to leave. Ma, have a hot lunch. It'll keep you warm."

"I have to go too. Be careful on your way home." Comrade Zhang left as well.

The blacksmith's wife, also a member of the network, brought me a bowl of hot noodles. After I was done, I bid them farewell and headed back to Kaifeng.

The snow had stopped and the ground was covered by a huge silver blanket. I imagined myself as a little ant moving slowly on the vast plain. From time to time, I crossed paths with other travellers on foot or in a horse-drawn cart. I looked over my shoulders often, but surreptitiously, to make sure I was not followed.

Halfway back to Kaifeng, two black dots behind me approached, gaining speed. They were two men about Wu's age. When they passed me, one of them stared at me for a few seconds too long and whispered something to the other. He, too, stared back at me. Then they walked on but slowed their speed considerably, keeping me in their line of vision. I got nervous. A little old lady travelling alone in such weather was indeed suspicious. What if they were spies for the enemy intending to report me at the city gate? A thorough pat-down may reveal the ID card in my jacket. I couldn't turn around and go back because that would be even more suspicious. The membership card had Wu's name on it, and it would not be hard for them to find out he was my son. I would never turn him in, but what if I got Xiao and Daisy in trouble, and even Master Chen?

I had to get rid of the card.

I looked around and saw a graveyard on my left. It was normal for travellers to hide behind a bush or among the *kurgans*, or mounds, of a graveyard to pee. I chose the moment the two men had their backs to me and used the last bit of energy hurrying to the graveyard.

I hid behind a kurgan, loosened the soil using my scissors and buried the card. The burial mound had a tombstone, but I couldn't read. I must remember this grave so one day we could retrieve it. The graves were scattered in a disorderly fashion. This one was near the centre. Just to make sure, I found a rock and placed it on the top of the kurgan. When I walked out, I pretended I had just peed and was fastening the belt of my pants.

As I guessed, the two men waited for me at the city gate. The guards questioned me about where I had gone. I told them I was visiting a sick relative out of town. They not only patted me down but rubbed the hems of my jacket inch by inch, finding nothing.

A week later, I figured it was safe for me to go back to the graveyard. I returned but could not find the spot where I buried Wu's party membership card. I hated myself and was mad with worry. Had I known how to read, I would have remembered the headstone. After three trips with no success, I had to tell Wu during our next meeting what had happened. He asked me not to worry, because if I couldn't find the card, he doubted anybody else could. Besides, he had already established contact with the cell in the blacksmith's place.

"Ma, I have something important to tell you." Wu grinned from ear to ear. I hadn't seen him so happy for a long time.

"What is it?"

"You see, Master Chen has a daughter, Snowflake, a nineteen-year-old nurse. It was she who nursed me back to health."

"In that case, we owe her a big favour," I said.

"Yes, and . . . and we plan to get married."

I couldn't believe my ears. Wu found himself a wife without a matchmaker or my approval. I didn't know what to say. Sensing my uneasiness, Wu said, "I'm sorry I didn't tell you sooner. It's not like we can meet often. She's very pretty and very kind. She will be a very good daughter-in-law, and I'm here asking for your approval."

When I thought of all the help Xiao and I had received from Master Chen, I believed Wu had made a good choice. It was wartime, and it was a new era. I should not expect my children to follow the traditions of our generation.

"Yes, I approve," I said.

"Great. Now, all we need is to get the approval from the network."

In the next year, I was only able to meet up with my son three times, each at a predetermined place far from both our neighbourhoods. He always disguised himself as an old man wearing a low straw hat. He did such a good job walking slowly, with a hunched back, that the first time I almost didn't recognize him. I asked him why he pretended to be old specifically. He told me the fake residential card the underground network got for him had belonged to an old man who had passed away, but his family didn't report his death to the authority. Instead, they allowed the network to use the man's card.

"We have more supporters than our enemies will ever know," Wu concluded. He then told me he had decided to stay in Kaifeng.

I questioned his decision. To me, working under the enemy's nose was too risky.

"I know. But I don't want to leave Snowflake. If I leave, God knows what will happen, and we may never see each other again."

The second time, we met at a riverbank. It was shortly after two Japanese soldiers were killed outside of the city walls. They had never caught the perpetrator.

We sat side by side, facing the river. He told me he and Snowflake had just gotten married.

"I'm so glad for you. Is there any way I can meet my daughter-in-law?' I asked.

"I'll ask my superior about it."

"I want to ask you something. Was the underground network responsible for the two dead Japanese?" I asked.

"No. Our mission is not to kill one or two Japanese," Wu said. "They were probably killed by ordinary Chinese, seeking revenge."

"What is your mission then?"

Wu lowered his voice to a whisper. "Our mission is to stay undercover for the long term while expanding the network, gathering intelligence on the higher-level officers in the Japanese army and in the puppet government, especially their spies."

"What if you bump into Qi?" I glanced around, seeing only a man sitting on the riverbank about fifty paces away with a fishing rod in his hand.

"First of all, Qi may not recognize me. I left home as a skinny boy and came back as an old man." My son winked at me. "Also, I'm not alone. Look at the man over there." He pointed his chin slightly in the direction of the fishing man. "He is a comrade, assigned to look out for me. Besides," he added, "I've been a spy before."

"Before? When? Where?"

"I was once sent on a mission with another comrade, Chang Cheng, to gather information behind the enemy lines. We hid in a small boat in the reeds. Someone had to go ashore to find food on a regular basis. Comrade Chang was too afraid, so I took over the responsibility. The mission was accomplished, and we returned unharmed." Wu grinned.

I didn't know what to say. How could Comrade Chang make my son take all the risk?

Being a spy was riskier than being in the army, but I

couldn't convince Wu to return. I guess eight horses wouldn't be able to pull a newly wed young man away.

The third time I met Wu, he was alone. We walked together on a quiet street.

"When could I meet your wife?" I looked around and saw a young woman about twenty paces away, carrying a flower basket.

"Ma, allow me to buy some flowers for you," Wu said.

I thought he was mad. We hardly had enough to eat. Who had the money for flowers?

He didn't wait for my reply and walked to the flower seller. I had to follow. When we stopped in front of the young woman, Wu said, "Ma, this is my wife, Snowflake."

"Please forgive me for not ketouing to you. I'm supposed to sell you flowers." She bent her knees slightly.

I was stunned, momentarily lost for words. This young woman wore a traditional, Chinese-style, light blue linen shirt with a high collar and three-quarter sleeves, a black muslin skirt to the knee, white socks and black, home-made cloth shoes—no embroidery designs, though. Her short hair just reached her earlobes. A jade bracelet dangled on each of her wrists. She looked like a student and was much prettier than I'd imagined.

"I'm so glad to meet you," I finally said.

Snowflake handed me a bundle of red peonies and whispered, "It's my honour to finally meet you, Mother." She emphasized the word *mother*. My heart was filled with love and gratitude. "We grow these in our courtyard." She winked at me.

I had never seen a daughter-in-law wink at her mother-in-law. In my generation, when a daughter-in-law met her in-laws, she ought to have her head bowed, eyes downcast and do as she was told. It seemed Snowflake was a carefree, modern girl.

My daughter-in-law walked away. She was like a beautiful snowflake falling from the sky right in front of me. When Wu and I were alone, I couldn't help but praise the woman he had chosen for a wife. Then I brought up the topic of returning to Shanbei again. I had this uneasy feeling. According to a well-known Chinese expression, the longer the night, the more nightmares.

"Ma." His eyes followed his wife's back without any facial expression. "I'm going to tell you something that you must promise never to share."

"Sure," I said.

"Shanbei is not as safe as you think." Wu sighed. "We all know Chiang Kai-shek's white terror killed tens of thousands of Communists—we were almost destroyed. But in Shanbei, we live in red terror. The party has gone through purge after purge. No one knows who will become the next target. One has to be very careful about what he says, when and to whom. Sometimes the things you say to your best friend are reported to the party. You don't know who the party spies are. Sometimes two comrades, or friends, or roommates, take a walk after supper, and one shoots the other when nobody is around. The deaths are never investigated because they were ordered from above."

Wu paused. "I'd rather be killed by the enemy than by my own comrades."

That sent a shiver down my spine.

Chapter 23

Not one drop of rain fell in the spring of 1942. All the wheat died before the grain filling period. By the summer, the ground cracked open under the sun, spreading out like a spider's web. When water was poured on the ground, it sizzled dry in seconds. Then locusts came. Billions of them swarmed over the farmlands, darkened the sky and left nothing in their path. In the stricken regions, millions of people starved to death. The survivors carried their children and belongings, fleeing to the west.

When farmers didn't have food, neither did city folks. Master Chen had to shut down his restaurant, and Xiao was unemployed. By 1943, the Japanese opened their military granaries and distributed rice and wheat flour through the *baojia* system to the residents.

When I received our first ration of rice, there was sand in it. Four ladles of the rice could wash out one inch of sand at the bottom of the woven basket. I was stunned that they mixed sand in wheat flour as well. One could wash the sand out of the rice, but with wheat flour it was impossible. The same happened to my neighbours. I assumed it was the Japanese who did this. But when Daisy told me her friends in the league received their rations without sand, I was puzzled.

"So who did this?" I asked.

"Who else? Who is our baozhang?" Daisy said.

"Qi," I said and realized what had happened. By pouring sand in the rations, he could easily siphon off a lot of grain from us. That bastard! But there was nothing we could do.

The famine lasted a year until the wheat harvest time the following summer. Rumour said millions starved to death, mostly in the countryside. I was worried about Orchid until I received a letter from her. Thank God she was fine.

On Daisy's eighteenth birthday, she informed me she had met a man in the league, and he had asked her to marry him.

"But you are only eighteen," I blurted out. The man, named Daniu—Big Ox—should have asked me for my daughter's hand. I was not a closed-minded person, but the new generation sometimes went too far. In addition, since Daisy returned home, I had been rethinking my relationship with Xiao. It was selfish to keep him by my side. I had thought of asking him to leave me and marry Daisy, but every time I started the conversation by saying I was too old for him, he would cut me off and wouldn't hear another word. If Daisy married Big Ox, Xiao would be all alone when I passed on.

"I need to think about it," I said.

"What is there to think about? Can't you see I stoop like an old woman? Who would want to marry me except Big Ox?"

"Fine, tell me about him," I said reluctantly.

"He is literate, and there's not a second person who

treats me as he does. We also have a lot to talk about."

"About what?"

"About the day when China becomes a democratic country, when government officials are not appointed by the powerful or bought with money but elected by the people. When that day comes, I'll run as a representative for the people."

Daisy's eyes had a dreamy light in them. I didn't know what to say. Xiao had done so much for me and for our family. With Daisy gone, there was no way I could repay him.

Six months later, Daisy and Big Ox got married. I asked Daisy to write to her sister about the big news, but she declined. Shortly after Daisy had returned home, we had received a letter from Orchid. In it, Orchid said her elder sister's decision to drop out of school was stupid. Since Daisy was the only one who could read, she was the one who read the letter for me and was obviously hurt. Orchid always spoke her mind. But Daisy was both sick and homesick at the time. How could I blame her for that? Since then, we hadn't received a single letter from Orchid, and Daisy refused to write to her sister too.

My son-in-law was nothing like a big ox. Instead, he had a small frame and looked fragile. As a peasant's son from Hubei province, he came to Kaifeng a few years earlier, seeking opportunities. Since he didn't have family in town, he moved in with us. I let the newlyweds live in the two-storey building. It was a separate courtyard, but I was still wary and ashamed. Xiao and I each had our own bedroom, only sharing a bed in the darkest time of the night. I also found Big Ox was a chatterbox. I only hoped he would never learn my deepest secret.

It was the summer of 1945. Daisy, Big Ox, Xiao and I had just finished supper when we heard shouting and the clanging of a gong. We ran out of our front gate. Four young men on a three-wheeled flat cart were beating a gong and shouting into a homemade paper trumpet, "The Japanese have surrendered! The Japanese have surrendered!"

Was this true? We looked at each other, unable to digest the news.

Daisy said, "Ma, it won't hurt to find out."

I locked our door, and we followed the cart. Along the way, more people emerged and followed the cart. When we arrived at Zhongshan Street, it was filled with people, bicycles, three-wheeled carts and even a few motorcars. A big banner hung from the window of Xinhua Bookstore.

"What does it say?" I asked.

"It says the Japanese have surrendered!" Daisy's eyes glistened with excitement.

Was this really happening? Eight years of blood, tears and humiliation. Eight years of being conquered subjects. The war was over? I was numb, not believing my ears. People danced around us, jumped up and down, mad with happiness. Newspaper kids shouted, "Special edition! Special edition! The Japanese have surrendered!"

People grabbed the newspapers from the children's hands and tossed coins at them. Some folks read the headlines aloud. The words rippled out, further and louder. Someone must have bought a stack of newspapers, for they tossed the bundles into the crowd. Hot tears ran down my face. I wiped them off, but they kept coming. Daisy cried until she hiccupped.

Like ocean waves, the compacted human bodies were gaining speed and surging forward.

Kids beat metal buckets and ran between the legs of adults. Unable to pass through the swarm, cars halted along the road. Red lanterns and banners hung above shop windows and doors. A skinny boy stood on the windowsill of Sea Dragon Drugstore, brandishing the national flag. Firecrackers erupted everywhere. A young man in tattered clothes climbed on the roof of a motorcar and shouted, "Let's sing a song!"

"Let's sing a song!" the crowd responded.

"Let's sing 'Marching On!'" he suggested.

"Marching on. Don't look back. This is the moment to sacrifice our lives . . ." People followed him. I didn't know how to sing, so I just clapped my hands. My children followed me. Then more people followed us. We clapped our hands to the rhythm of the song. I never knew I had the power to influence others.

A huge banner with four portraits appeared above the crowd. Chiang Kai-shek's portrait was one, along with those of three foreigners.

"Who are they?" I asked Daisy.

"Leaders of our allies." Daisy pointed at a portrait of a man with bushy brows and a thick moustache. "That's Stalin, leader of Russia."

"How do you know?"

"Their names are written underneath."

My illiteracy had made me a dummy.

Big Ox pointed at the second one from the left. "That's the president of the United States. And the one next to Chiang Kai-shek is the prime minister of England."

"Ma," Daisy shouted over the noise. "Where is Wu? He doesn't need to hide anymore."

Indeed. Now that the Japanese were defeated, Wu could come home.

"Let's go home. Maybe Wu is there waiting for us," I shouted.

Wu didn't come home until the next morning, along with Snowflake. She looked even more lovely. It seemed all the joy in the world rushed into my heart at once, which couldn't contain so much happiness and it spilled to my smiling face.

After lunch, Wu suggested it was time for me to meet with Snowflake's mother.

"You are right," I said. Not only had they saved Wu's life, but they also gave their daughter to him. I owed them so much.

Xiao, Daisy, Big Ox and I went to Master Chen's restaurant the next day for a banquet. Mrs. Chen was a petite woman around my age. Her grey hair was coiffed in a bun. I could see Snowflake's features in her.

It was after business hours. Wu and Snowflake sat next to each other. Mrs. Chen sat beside me. After we greeted each other, I wanted to say a few words to thank the couple, but a strand of warmness rose in my chest and blocked my throat. I was suddenly at a loss for words.

Mrs. Chen started the conversation, "Mrs. Li, you have so many grown-up children. I envy you. Snowflake is our only child."

"But your daughter is the pearl in the ocean and the star in the sky. My son must have accumulated enough virtue in his previous life to have such a wife." I didn't know where those clever words came from.

Everybody smiled. Snowflake blushed.

"Don't you think all your children will be home soon?" Mrs. Chen asked.

"I hope so," I said.

"It's not that simple," Wu sighed. "The civil war has already begun, and I'll have to leave soon."

"But the Nationalists and the Communists are having peace talks," Master Chen said.

"They are only pretending to have peace talks. We are enemies. Both parties are trying to gain time to prepare for the war," Wu said.

"Where will you go?" I asked Wu.

"I have received orders to report to another city. I won't know the details until I get there."

"What about Qi? Shouldn't he be punished now?" I asked.

"I'm sure he will be, but we have to deal with the Nationalists first," Wu said.

As a member of the Underground Communists' Network, I knew I shouldn't ask much. So, instead of my other children coming home, Wu was leaving.

I still had Daisy by my side.

Civil War

KAIFENG CITY,
HENAN PROVINCE

1945–1949

Chapter 24

Wu left Kaifeng a week later. He told me he would be in Zhengxian City and work as a spy in the Nationalist Army.

"But how are you going to get inside?" I asked.

"Under a fake name and ID. It has all been arranged."

On the day of Wu's departure, Snowflake cried her eyes into two spoiled peaches. In the following weeks, she often came to my house and helped me with household chores. The love we shared for the same man bound us together and I found myself more and more attached to my daughter-in-law.

Three and a half months later, Wu suddenly returned home. I couldn't believe my eyes. The man in front of me had the most fashionable wavy hairdo held up by hair gel. Dressed in a grey western suit and a tie, looking nice but borrowed, he should have never shown up at my front door. Something must be wrong.

"What happened?" I asked.

"I must leave Henan as soon as possible. Yesterday I received an order from my upstream contact, asking me to warn my downstream contact that he had been exposed and was about to be arrested. I ran all the way to his place, only to see him being taken away by the Nationalist soldiers. I immediately hid on a street corner. The comrade turned his head in my direction, but I'm not sure if he saw me. I reported this to the spy network. This morning, I was ordered to leave immediately, just in case my contact talks under torture."

"Where will you go?" I asked.

"I don't know. There's no time for the network to make any arrangements. I was told to just leave Henan, to anywhere I choose, and wait for further instruction. Where can I go?"

The only place I could think of was Big Ox's hometown, in Hubei province. I told Wu. "Have you seen your wife yet? Is she in danger?"

"Not yet. She is not in danger. Remember, no one knows we are married."

"Let's talk to Big Ox, but you can't wear this on the run. It's too noticeable," I said.

"I know. I planned to change here," Wu said.

We told Big Ox and Daisy what had happened.

"No problem," Big Ox said. "I'll write an introductory letter to my family for Wu. They live in a village. Nobody cares about who is coming and going."

I found an old shirt and a pair of pants that were Xiao's, asked Wu to change and went to see Number 308.

"What's wrong?" Number 308 asked. "You look terrible." I told him.

"But we don't have enough money to buy a train ticket." I hated to ask for help.

"Just wait here." He left the room and soon returned with a few wrinkled bills. "This should be enough for a train ticket."

"I'll pay you back," I said.

"Don't mention it. Go and get your son out of town."

Wu looked like a labourer in Xiao's clothes. I quickly messed up his hair and handed the money to him. "Now, go tell your wife," I said.

The next day, Wu appeared at my doorstep again.

"What happened?"

"Snowflake wants to go with me."

I couldn't believe this. Wu was running for his life. What was Snowflake thinking? A vacation?

I held back my frustration. "But I only borrowed enough money for one ticket." I couldn't go back to Number 308. "She'll just have to wait for you to come back. If you must, ask your father-in-law to reason with his daughter."

"Master Chen has already talked to her. It's no use."

Based on my years of experience as an underground messenger, every minute counted. I rubbed my palms and felt the ring on my finger. I stopped and looked at the plain gold ring. My wedding ring! It had never left my finger, even when we were starving.

I took the ring to a pawn shop and got enough money for a second train ticket and to repay Number 308.

After the Japanese retreated, the Nationalists dug trenches outside the city and made the land bare within two hundred metres of Kaifeng's city walls, making it impossible for an attacking army to hide. They also made small trenches in the major crossroads in the city.

The war between the Communists and the Nationalists had now been raging for three years. We'd grown accustomed to hearing gunfire and bombing east of the city. I prayed every day for the Communists to come because it meant I would see Wen and Wu again.

The fifth day of the fifth month of the lunar calendar was the Dragon Boat Festival, to commemorate Qu Yuan[16]. For the festival of 1948, folks in Kaifeng made *zongzi*, deep-fried sticky rice cakes and sweet chips, hung sage bushes above their doors and made their children wear *wu du xie*[17].

As Daisy, Big Ox, Xiao and I sat down to eat zongzi, we heard bang, bang, bang—much louder than gunfire. Bombshells? We ran to the courtyard, then to the street. People shouted, "The Eighth Route Army is here! The Communists are here!"

The Communists! The day I had been waiting for so long. "What do we do?" I asked my children.

"Remember what Master Chen said," Xiao reminded

---

[16] Qu Yuan (340–278 BC) was a patriotic poet and advisor in the court of Chu during the Warring States period of ancient China who was exiled by the emperor for perceived disloyalty. Qu Yuan had proposed a strategic alliance with the state of Qi in order to fend off the threatening state of Qin, but the Chu emperor didn't believe it and sent Qu Yuan off to the wilderness. Unfortunately, Qu Yuan was right about the threat presented by Qin, which soon captured and imprisoned the emperor. The next king of Chu surrendered the state to their rivals. Upon hearing the tragic news, Qu Yuan, in 278 BC, drowned himself in the Miluo River, in Hunan Province. The Chu state was shadowed with grief. Fishers rowed along the river to find his body, while others threw cooked rice balls into the river, believing that when the fish were fed they would not eat Qu Yuan's body. Gradually, rowing developed into dragon boat racing and rice balls became zongzi—sticky rice wrapped in a pyramid shape using bamboo or reed leaves—and passed down from generation to generation as a Chinese tradition.

[17] *wu du xie*: shoes usually embroidered with a tiger's head, a symbol to prevent harm from scorpions, snakes, geckos, centipedes and toads.

me. "When the battle starts, we can all go to their place and hide in their underground tunnel."

"But they live in the southwest—"

Xiao grabbed me by the shoulders. "What choice do we have?"

He was right. Even though walking across the city was dangerous, staying in our house was worse. A bomb could hit the house and burn us alive.

My tiny feet and Daisy's injured back meant neither of us could run. Xiao put me on his back, Big Ox carried Daisy on his back and we left home.

As we travelled, gunfire and bombs exploded. The acrid smell of smoke filled my nostrils, reminding me of our escape ten years ago when Kaifeng was attacked by the Japanese. The scorching sun beat down on our weary backs as the salty sweat ran into my mouth. At last, we made it to Master Chen's door.

"We've been waiting for you." Master Chen quickly ushered us inside and to the backyard. When he lifted the lid of the tunnel entrance, a ladder appeared. I halted. Women with bound feet had to walk on their heels. To place my heels on the narrow ladder steps accurately and firmly was nothing short of walking a tightrope. How was I supposed to do it?

Master Chen saw my hesitation. "Don't worry. It's only seven steps. My wife is already down there. If she can climb a ladder, you can too," he said, climbing down ahead of me.

With shaky legs, I gingerly placed my right heel on the ladder step, then the left heel. Sweat broke out and made my hands slippery. A sudden fatigue overwhelmed me.

"You're doing fine," Master Chen shouted from the bottom. "Don't be afraid. If you fall off, I'm here to catch you." Xiao and Big Ox lay flat on their bellies, extending their upper bodies over the opening from above so they were able to press their hands on top of mine and move with them as I inched down. Little by little, I was finally lowered into the tunnel.

We had to crouch and sit on the ground, shoulder to shoulder. Master Chen pulled the lid shut, plunging us into total darkness.

"Don't worry. We have candles here when needed." Mrs. Chen's voice came from the far side of the tunnel.

Even though outside the sun was relentless, the tunnel was cool and damp. I wrinkled my nose against the strong smell of mould and had difficulty breathing. *When a person is dead and buried, it must feel like this.* Then I wanted to laugh. How could a dead person feel?

"Don't worry about food and water," Master Chen reassured us. "We have a pile of sweet potatoes and a bucket of water stored here. It should last us a few days."

"What if we need to go to the washroom?" Daisy asked.

"You'll have to go outside," Mrs. Chen said.

My stomach flip-flopped. Would I have to climb the ladder again?

In the tunnel, we spent most of the time in silence. After hours of sitting in one position, my legs and feet were numb. When I tried to move them, it felt like they were stabbed by a thousand needles. At night, my feet were burning hot and pulsing. I could hardly fall asleep. When I finally did, I had nightmares about falling off the ladder.

Life was harsh, especially for women. I was so tired that sometimes I just wanted to close my eyes and fall into a deep sleep, never to wake up. But not now, not yet, not before I saw all my children again.

When I closed my eyes, I could see Wen as a teenager—the thick hair and inky brows. His eyes always showed determination. It had been eleven years since he and Wu left home. Was he in the attacking army just outside the city? Would I see him soon?

How were Wu and Snowflake faring? Were they safe? Were they caught in the crossfire? I had received a letter from Zhong recently; he and his wife planned to leave Xi'an City for southern China, to make a living in his wife's hometown. So my eldest son was not coming home. The last time I saw him was at Luoyang's train station ten years earlier. Kaifeng was not too far from Xi'an. They could have come to see me before leaving for Guangdong, but they didn't. I could only weep in Xiao's arms.

When Orchid had graduated from First National High School, she had finally written. She was on her way to Xi'an to seek shelter at Zhong's place while she prepared for the university entrance exam. In the year the Japanese surrendered, she had passed the exam and became a college student. The first college student in our family—I was so proud of her! A few months later, though, we received another letter from her, informing us she was married to a college teacher in a small town not far from Xi'an. As to why she dropped out of college and got married, she didn't say. The next thing I knew, they had a daughter. My baby had a baby already? It was hard to believe. The last time I saw her was the morning of May 23, 1938, when she and Daisy left home for school and didn't come back. She was only eleven years old. She could have come home after the Japanese surrendered. Perhaps it was the civil war. No one wanted to be caught in the crossfire.

Did the children know how much a mother had to endure without seeing them for so long?

We hid in the tunnel for a week, surviving on sweet potatoes. The bucket of water lasted us only two days. Xiao and Big Ox took turns climbing out to fetch more for us.

The worst was going out to relieve myself. Only with Xiao pulling from above and Big Ox pushing from underneath could I manage to climb out of that hole. I had held my bladder for so long that when I finally let go, I couldn't pee for the first few seconds. What if a bomb fell on me while I was relieving myself? I wouldn't want to die with my trousers down.

Outside, the familiar smell of gunpowder and burnt wood reminded me of the Japanese bombing. But this time, the Chinese were killing the Chinese. It didn't make any sense.

On the eighth day, the bombing and gunfire stopped. We waited for a long while before climbing out. I gulped in fresh air like a fish that had just been thrown back in the water. We patted off the dust on our clothes, gingerly opened the front gate and stuck our heads out. Other than black smoke in the distance, we saw no soldiers.

"The Nationalist Army is defeated! The Eighth Route Army is here!" We could hear voices shouting.

The battle was over.

After we washed and fed ourselves, we rushed out to

Zhongshan Street to watch the Eighth Route Army marching into the city. They came from the east and south gates in single file. Their faces were muddy, sweaty and without emotion. Their uniforms were not any better than our clothing. The things that marked them as soldiers were their guns and puttees. Pockets of fires still burned here and there. The soldiers dispersed in groups to help residents put out the fires. A small guy leading a group carried a red flag with five golden stars—a big one in the centre and four small ones surrounding it. He looked so tired, it seemed he could drop and fall asleep at any time. I had thought they would sing songs and march in formations.

So this was *our* army—an army I'd sewed for, carried secret messages for and risked my life for. An army to which I had given two of my sons. I wanted to offer them food and water but couldn't risk missing my son. I looked closely at each sweaty, black, ash-covered face, looking for Wen. Eleven years would have turned a boy into a man. Still, I would recognize him. He was a copy of Wu, and he was my son.

The Eighth Route Army soon left Kaifeng and marched to other battlefields. Wen didn't show up. The former Eighth Route Army had changed its name to the People's Liberation Army and had grown to over one million soldiers. They were on their way to liberate southern China.

Patience, I told myself. *All I need is patience.* I was sure my son would come home one day.

∽⦿⌒

"Liberation"

KAIFENG CITY, HENAN PROVINCE-
MAIXIANG TOWN, SHAANXI PROVINCE

1949–1952

∽⦿⌒

Chapter 25

Now that China was liberated, I looked forward to Wu and Snowflake's return. One day in October, just after lunch, I heard loud knocks on our front gate. I hurried to the front courtyard. There they were, Wu and Snowflake, with two toddlers, a boy and a girl.

I rushed to them and almost fell. "My God, is this you, my son?"

Wu caught me in his arms. "Be careful, Ma."

Daisy also came out of the house, stooped like an old woman. Big Ox followed her.

"Brother, sister-in-law!" Daisy cried.

I scanned Wu from head to toe. He was even darker but seemed healthy and strong. Snowflake was a little rounder and had a motherly look in her eyes.

"Ma, please accept your daughter-in-law's curtsy." Snowflake bent her knees slightly and turned to the children. "Star, Moon, this is your grandma. Say, 'Nai nai.'"

"Nai nai," they said shyly.

"They're twins," Wu said.

These were the most beautiful words I had ever heard. But soon the children turned their attention to Daisy. They looked at her inquisitively; then Star called her nai nai as well.

We all laughed, except Daisy.

Snowflake scolded the boy. "Silly boy, this is your auntie."

"Auntie," the boy said in a small voice.

I felt sorry for Daisy. If not for her stooped posture, the boy wouldn't have mistaken her for a grandmother.

"Don't stand there." I grabbed Snowflake's hands. "Come in! Have you eaten?"

"Yes, we have eaten at my parents' house."

Once we were sitting around the stove in our guest hall and Big Ox had poured tea for everyone, I said, "Tell me everything about your exile."

Wu started, "Being a peasant isn't so bad. I laboured in the fields during the day. Snowflake cooked and cleaned and looked after the children. The work was hard, but I didn't have to look over my shoulder all the time. The past three years have been the most peaceful time in my life."

Wu moved to the edge of his chair. "Tell us about your life in the past three years. I bet Qi has been punished by the Communists."

"On the contrary. One would think after the Japanese surrendered that any war traitor would have become the object of universal condemnation. Like in the Chinese phrase, when a rat crosses the street, everyone shouts to kill it. But Qi is not just anyone. Even though he himself hardly showed his face in public, his wife started to work for the Communists as a grassroots activist. After the liberation, she must have secured her husband's safety. No one has touched him."

"It is so unfair. What an upside-down world!" Wu cried out.

"Yes, it is unfair. But what can we do? Nothing. As long as all my children are safe and sound, I'm happy," I said.

That evening, when Xiao came home from work, my life felt almost perfect. Out of my five children, two were with me. I had also gained a son-in-law, a daughter-in-law and two grandchildren.

We had a big supper together. When Wu realized we still fed on sweet potatoes and leftovers from Master Chen's restaurant, he said, "I will report to the government tomorrow as a Communist Party member and a veteran. I'm sure they will give me a job."

I realized now I had someone to rely on. Wu sounded and acted like the head of the family, much more capable and strong than Xiao and Big Ox combined.

Wu reported to the government. The next day, a sack of wheat flour was delivered to our home. Even though I had lost Wu's party membership card in the graveyard a few years earlier, with the reference letter provided by the underground network, Wu was able to get a job as a captain in Kaifeng's armed police force.

Wu came home wearing the police uniform with a handgun holstered in his belt. I felt safe for the first time in a long time. By tradition, Wu and his family should live with me. They agreed. If only my other three children were here, my shattered family would be whole again.

A month after starting his new job, Wu came home from work looking downtrodden. "Ma, the party is about to punish all those who once served in the Nationalist government or had anything to do with them."

"How does that have anything to do with us?" I asked.

Wu sunk into a chair in the living room. "Have you forgotten that Big Ox is a member of the Three Principles Youth League?"

I stared at him, not able to think for a moment. Then I remembered. "Big Ox told me it was an anti-Japanese organization. Many young people joined it during the war."

"It was established by Chiang Kai-shek, and he is the enemy of the Communists. That's why the League is classified as a counter-revolutionary organization. No doubt they'll be punished."

"How?"

Wu shook his head. "I don't know. Arrest, jail time or even worse!"

"What are we going to do?" I asked.

"Let's talk about it with Daisy and Big Ox tonight."

We held a family meeting that evening. I learned the three principles were the principles of nationalism, democracy, and the people's livelihood. I didn't see anything wrong with it.

"How about the traitors like Qi? Why are the Communists not punishing them?" I asked.

"We're just ordinary citizens, not the decision-makers. There's no point in discussing it." Wu turned to Big Ox and Daisy. "I know how the Communists operate. Their punishments are swift and hard. If you want to have a chance in life, you need to run."

Big Ox's face turned paper white. "Where should we go?"

"Go back to Hubei," Wu suggested. "You sent us there. Now it's your turn. Settle down as peasants. As long as you don't reveal your identities, nobody will know your history."

What had this world become? Those who fought against the Japanese had to run, but those who served the enemies did not suffer any punishment.

Three days later, I said goodbye to Daisy and Big Ox at the train station. I had seen Wen and Wu leave from this station many years ago, then Wu and Snowflake, now Daisy and Big Ox. It seemed we always had to run from something. When China was liberated, I thought we didn't have to run anymore. How wrong I was.

As the train disappeared from my view, the hope in my heart also dissipated.

The winter of 1950 came sooner than usual. It was only November, and we already had heavy snow. One day, Wu didn't come home for supper. I thought he might have to work overtime again, so I left his supper in the kitchen and went to sleep. The next morning before I got up, Snowflake knocked on my door.

"Wu didn't come home last night." Her bloodshot eyes were wide and panicky.

"Go to the police station to look for him, then," I said.

By mid-morning, Snowflake came home crying. "Ma, Wu has been arrested."

"What?" I grabbed her hands. "Who arrested him? For what?"

"The order was from the police chief. Wu is accused of being a traitor."

I knew my son. There was no way he was a traitor. There must be a mistake. "Take me to the police station," I demanded.

A police major was kind enough to meet with us. He was

a big man with a dark red face. People called him Major Double-Guns because he could shoot with two pistols at the same time, one in each hand.

"I'm Li Wu's mother. I heard my son was arrested. What is the charge?" I asked the man behind the desk.

"Mrs. Li, the order came from our new police chief. I don't know the details, and I can't help. We just carry out the orders." Major Double-Guns spread his hands, palms up.

"Where is he held?" Snowflake asked.

"Kaifeng Prison," the major said and stood up. "Show the guests out," he shouted to the guard outside the room.

We had to leave.

"We need to go to the prison to see him," Snowflake said.

I looked at my daughter-in-law's young face and swollen eyes. What kind of life had Wu given her? When they first met, Wu had to hide from the Japanese and look over his shoulder all the time. Then Wu left home and worked as a spy in Zhengxian. Next, they had to make a run to Hubei. Now this.

"Yes, let's do that," I said.

We arrived at the prison and told the guards our intentions but were refused.

"No visiting allowed. That's the order."

The guards' bayonets glistened in the cold wind. I looked at those twenty-something kids and thought, *You little bastards, you still smell of your mother's milk. I sewed for you in the wee hours of the night, under the dining table draped with a quilt. I risked my life carrying secret messages for you and your party. I saw you as my own sons. And now you pretend you don't know me.* I wanted to tear up my flesh, show them my heart: the heart of a mother, an old woman who had sent her three sons to the battlefields to fight the Japanese. I almost did it but checked myself. I couldn't go mad. I needed a clear mind to save my son.

"Let's go home for now," Snowflake tugged my sleeve. "There has to be a way."

Chapter 26

Worrying about Wu, I didn't sleep much and had to drag myself out of bed.

Puffy snow covered everything. Icicles decorated trees and eaves. Someone knocked loudly on our front gate. Xiao was a few steps ahead of me and opened it.

Three people stood at the door. Leading the pack was Qi's pock-faced wife, much heavier now. A man with a big belly and meaty hands stood at her right. I recognized him as the man from the Li clan who had conspired with Qi so many years ago to steal my husband's estate and stop me from burying him. I blinked, couldn't believe what I was seeing. Why were they here? Having a hard-core traitor husband, Qi's wife dared to show her face in public? China had been liberated. I shouldn't be afraid of them anymore. But Wu had just been arrested. I had to be careful. A third man I didn't know stood at her left.

"You are here—"

With a straight face, my stepdaughter-in-law said, "You can call me Comrade Chair, as I'm the chair of our newly formed Street Committee."

"What fragrant breeze has blown you here, Comrade Chair?" I asked sarcastically. By now, Snowflake had come out of the room. She and Xiao stood by my side.

Pock-face took out a folded piece of paper from her pocket, smoothed it out and read, "The eviction notice from the People's Government of Kaifeng. Because Li Wu has been arrested and convicted as a traitor to the Eighth Route Army, the property belonging to Li Wu and his mother Hu Jinfeng—Number 20 Sunshine Street—is therefore confiscated by the people's government. The residents of this property are ordered to move out immediately."

"No! This can't be true!" Stars exploded in front of my eyes. Xiao and Snowflake held me on each side, preventing me from falling.

Pock-face thrust the piece of paper to me. "Read it yourself."

Snowflake took it and scanned it quickly.

"Mother, it's true," she said in a shaking voice.

"But it is my house, not Wu's. My husband built it for our family!" I yelled. This was daylight robbery. How could they do this to me? Was there no law?

"Your house, Li Wu's house, it makes no difference. As a traitor's family, you are ordered to move out." The evil woman crossed her arms.

"Traitor? Who is the traitor? When the Japanese—"

Xiao stopped me in time. "But to where?"

Comrade Chair handed me another piece of paper. "Number 3 Liberation Street. Not the house, but the tool shed in the backyard. The monthly rent is fifty cents, due on the first of every month. You need to come to the Street Committee's office to pay it."

A tool shed, and they would charge us rent for it? I

stared at her in disbelief. Was this the government my children and I had risked our lives for? They were not any better than the Nationalists, perhaps worse.

"Why do we need to rent somebody else's tool shed when we have our own?" Snowflake asked.

Comrade Chair frowned. "Because we don't want you to cause any conflict with the new residents."

"What new residents?" Would it be Qi? No, it couldn't be. He had already taken a house from us. As a hard-core traitor during the war, how dare he take another?

"Stop asking questions! You need to vacate the premises by five o'clock this afternoon." Comrade Chair brushed some snow off her sleeves and turned on her heels.

"Five o'clock today!" The fat ruffian shouted and they followed the witch out.

My legs buckled as Snowflake caught me.

"Let me go! How can this be?" I pushed her away, dropped myself on the snowy ground and wailed. I was sure Qi had something to do with this.

Xiao and Snowflake half-lifted, half-dragged me inside. When Star and Moon saw we were crying, they began to cry too.

"The children and I can move back to my parents' home," Snowflake said, "but—"

"Don't worry about us," Xiao said. "We'll move to the tool shed."

The land deeds! I had to take them with me. As long as I held onto them, I could prove that this property belonged to our family. As for the hidden treasures, I didn't have time or space to move the jar. I had to leave them behind. They were safer in their hidden place than being dug out.

Xiao said, "I'll go to the restaurant and tell Master Chen what happened. I'll ask for a day off."

I nodded.

By five o'clock, Snowflake and the children had moved back to her parents' house. Xiao loaded a few pieces of furniture, some pots and pans and our clothes onto a pushcart. I put the land deeds in the inner pocket of my cotton-padded winter jacket. Before we left the house, I had one last look around. This was the house my husband built for the Li family, for generations to come. I had finally lost it, not to the Japanese, not to the Nationalists, not to Qi, but to the Communists.

My eyes stung with hot tears.

Xiao and I moved into the shed that afternoon. Only on October 1 of the previous year, Chairman Mao had announced from the tower on Tiananmen Square that the Chinese people had finally stood up, yet now we were brought to our knees.

Chapter 27

I fell sick the next day and stayed in bed, in the shack, for two weeks. I knew Snowflake came and went, bringing us food. Xiao stayed by my side, spoon-feeding me. When I was better, Xiao told me that ten families had moved into my five-courtyard house, including Qi. But he already had a stand-alone courtyard all to himself. Why did he want to share with others? Then it dawned on me that he was there for the treasure. I couldn't die yet. I had a son to save and scores to settle with Qi.

When Orchid appeared on my doorstep, I couldn't believe my eyes. She was taller than me, had a slender figure and was dressed neatly. For twelve years I hadn't seen her. My baby, my sweet baby.

"Is this really you, Orchid?" Tears ran down my face like little creeks.

Orchid sat on the edge of my bed, holding my hands with hers. "Yes, Mother, it's me. I sent you a letter in advance. Haven't you received it?"

"No. I have not received any letters." I was not surprised that no one forwarded the letter to me.

"I went to our house and was told you moved out. What's going on?"

I gave her a brief version of what had happened to us. "You must save your brother. Wu has been arrested," I said at the end.

"Auntie, sister Orchid perhaps needs some food and water first," Xiao said.

"Of course," I said. Xiao boiled some water and cooked a simple meal for Orchid. We didn't have anything other than a bit of green bean flour and a few potatoes.

"Is there anyone in the party who can help with Wu's case?" Orchid asked.

"Number 308 may be able to help," Xiao said.

Number 308. Yes. How could I have forgotten him? I quickly told Orchid who 308 was.

"It's worth a try," Orchid said.

I realized my youngest daughter had grown into a cool-headed, intelligent young woman.

"You must be tired," I said. "Have a good sleep tonight and we will go to 308 first thing tomorrow morning."

We had two single beds in our shed. In fact, they were just two pieces of plywood set up on long stools. I had to send Xiao to Master Chen's home to sleep when Orchid was there.

The next morning, Orchid and I paid 308 a visit. His hair had turned snow white. We hadn't seen each other since the Japanese surrendered five years earlier. I told him why we were there.

"You've been working for the Communists for ages. You must know someone who can help," I pleaded.

He thought for a moment. "Let me talk to Double-Gun. I'll go to him right now."

We thanked the man profusely.

When we got home, Snowflake was already there waiting for us. This was the first time Snowflake and Orchid met. By suppertime, 308 came and told us he had permission from Double-Gun to let us visit Wu. However, only one visitor was allowed. He handed us a note from Double-Gun and told us to show it to the guards.

"How am I going to repay you?" I said.

"No need. I'm sure if I were in trouble, you would do the same for me."

How I longed to catch a glimpse of my son. However, when I met Snowflake's eyes gleaming with anticipation, I had to give this only opportunity to her, as Wu's wife. I pressed the note from Double-Gun into her hand. "Make sure you don't lose it, and you must find out the real reason for his arrest."

The next morning, Xiao, Orchid and I accompanied Snowflake all the way to the prison gate. Snowflake showed the note to the guards. She was let in.

The stone walls of the prison were twice a man's height. Glass shards embedded on top of the walls sparkled in the sunlight. The air felt chilly, and I pulled my cotton-padded winter jacket tighter. This prison was once used by the Japanese to lock up anti-Japanese fighters, and later used by the Nationalists to lock up the Communists along with common criminals. Now the Communists used it on their own. I looked at the top of the wall. On the other side was my son, Orchid's brother whom she hadn't seen for twelve years. Would we ever see him again? We were so close, and yet so far apart. I wished I were a real phoenix so I could fly over the walls, carry my son on my back and fly away.

While waiting for Snowflake to come out, I asked Orchid if she had ever received the telegram from me while she was in Hankou and I was in Luoyang so many years ago.

"Yes, I did, and I mailed a letter with ten *yuan* for you and Xiao to buy train tickets to come to Hankou. Why didn't you ever come?"

"Ten yuan? I never received any letters or money from you in Luoyang. What was the address you used?" I asked.

Orchid admitted that she had put my name and Luoyang Refugee Camp on the envelope. Obviously, the letter and money were lost or taken. Had I received the money, my daughters and I would have had a reunion in Hankou twelve years ago. Xiao and I wouldn't have had to return home; Daisy wouldn't have returned home either and suffered the injury, and I wouldn't have been raped by the Japanese. But that also meant when Wu was injured, I wouldn't have been there for him. Fate, I realized, was totally out of our hands.

When Snowflake came out, her eyes were red and puffy.

"How is he?" we asked at the same time.

"He's handcuffed and his ankles are locked with fetters as if he is a dangerous criminal! When he walked, I could hear the chain being dragged on the floor. They didn't even let me into the cell. We spoke through a small aperture in the door."

"What did he tell you?" I asked.

Orchid interjected. "Let's get home and talk."

Back at the shed, Snowflake told us what Wu had learned about his arrest. When he worked as a spy in Zhengxian, one of his contacts was arrested by the Nationalists. The comrade survived and after the liberation, he became the new police chief in Kaifeng and found out Wu worked in the same police force. He accused Wu of selling him out to the Nationalists years before.

"That's not true!" I cried out. "Wu told me what happened back then. He had been sent to help this person flee but arrived at the comrade's street just in time to see him being taken away from his house. That's why Wu had to flee too, for fear of the comrade speaking under torture.

"Obviously it was a misunderstanding," Orchid exclaimed. "Did Wu tell the authorities what really happened?"

Snowflake nodded. "Of course. But the police chief doesn't believe him."

"Where is the person who gave Wu the order? All we need is his testimony," Orchid said.

"Wu told me he died three months ago," Snowflake sighed.

No! There must be a way. I couldn't let hope slip from my grasp.

"How about others? A network must have more than one person," Orchid asked.

My daughter knew nothing about how the network worked. I told her about the *dan xian lian xi* protocol. For example, 308 passed orders to me. I was 309, and the only other person I knew was 310. Should I be arrested and tortured, only 308 and 310 were in danger and needed to flee. The entire network would not be discovered. In Wu's case, of the only two people he knew, one accused him of being a traitor, and the other was dead.

"It's not fair," Xiao grunted.

"But nobody can prove he is guilty either," Orchid said.

"The police chief claims that he himself is the proof," Snowflake said. "Because when he was being taken away, he saw Wu with his own eyes hiding on the street corner. Other questions were raised, too, such as why Wu was the sole survivor of his platoon when they were bombed by the Japanese many years ago. How could he be so lucky? He must have led the Japanese bombers to the platoon's location. Also, Wu claims he was a party member, but he has no proof. He doesn't have a party membership card."

It was as if someone had struck me. I cried out, "It was all my fault. I lost it in the graveyard." I told them about taking the assignment to help Wu connect with the underground radio station and how I lost his membership card.

"But there must be someone he once worked with, someone who knew him and can prove his party member status and that he's a good, loyal Communist," Orchid said.

Snowflake said, "Wu said the only person who can save him is Chang Cheng, a vice-minister now. Wu used to work with him behind enemy lines. One letter from him can verify that Wu is a good and loyal Communist."

"Wu told me about this comrade!" I said. "When the two of them hid in a boat in a reedy swamp, it was Wu who went out to get food and water every day. Chang Cheng was too afraid. As far as I see it, this fellow owes Wu a huge favour. But where can we find him?"

Snowflake retrieved a piece of paper from her inside pocket. "Wu wrote a letter to Chang Cheng. The address is on the back. We must deliver this letter in person, because if the letter is lost in the mail, Wu may die."

Orchid read the lines on the back of the letter out loud, "To Chengdu City, Sichuan Province, Southwest Economic Bureau, Vice-Minister Chang Cheng. But there is no street name and number."

"Wu said all we need to find is the building of the provincial government," Snowflake said. "The staff will lead us to him."

I felt as if I was sitting on a swing. One moment I was dropped to the bottom; the next moment I was thrust to the sky.

"Who will go?" Orchid asked.

"I will," I said.

Orchid glanced at my bound feet. "It's a very long trip, about a sixteen-hour train ride."

"Xiao and I walked all the way from Kaifeng to Luoyang. I can handle a train ride," I told her.

Snowflake came by my side. "We will go together, and I can look after Mother on the way."

Orchid also wanted to go with us, but I stopped her. She had been coughing for the last few days. Even though she said it was nothing, I didn't want her to get sicker on the way.

Orchid went out the next morning and bought a twenty-five-kilo sack of wheat flour and some pork, and hired a coolie who carried the load home. We made twenty steamed pork buns for the trip.

That afternoon, we said goodbye to Orchid and Xiao at the train station.

Chapter 28

Snowflake and I boarded the train. We didn't have money to buy berth tickets, but at least we had legitimate tickets. The memory of being thrown out of a train years ago made me nervous. I clutched the ticket in my pocket till my hand was sweaty, as if I relaxed my grip for even a moment, it would fly away.

We put our small bundle on the luggage rack and managed to find one seat. Most people had to stand in the aisle. Snowflake insisted I sit. Fortunately, after three stops, someone got off the train and Snowflake was able to sit down as well. The landscape sped by but I wasn't in the mood to appreciate it.

People sitting around me dozed off, but I couldn't fall asleep. Images of Wu's childhood flickered across my mind. He and Wen almost looked identical, but Wu was an inch taller than Wen. Wen kept things to himself and was quiet most of the time. In contrast, Wu liked to talk and was more daring. Could this trip save his life? What if we couldn't find the vice-minister? It felt as if twenty-five mice were inside of me—a hundred paws clawing at my heart.

We ate some of the buns. I hadn't had meat since we

were kicked out of our house, and I savoured the pork stuffing. Snowflake went to the dinner cart to fill up our water canteen. We didn't talk much—too many ears nearby.

It was snowing when we arrived in Chengdu the next day. We found a small hotel near the train station. The money Orchid had given me was only enough for three nights. If we couldn't find Chang Cheng in three days, there was no backup plan.

Snowflake approached the counter. "We want a room."

The owner was a man in his forties with a small red nose. He said something we didn't understand. His language sounded foreign to me. He had to be speaking a local dialect.

"One room." I showed my index finger.

"Your residential card," Red Nose said. This time I understood.

We presented our residential cards and were ushered into a room. I collapsed on the bed, my feet cold and numb.

A middle-aged woman came in with a bucket of water and two towels. She pointed at the wash basin on a metal stand and another wash basin underneath the bed, and left. I understood her only by her gesture. My God, did everyone here speak only the dialect? I hoped the government people spoke a language we understood.

We washed our faces and feet. Snowflake went to the front, to find out where the provincial government building was. She came back with a hand-drawn map.

"If we hire a rickshaw, it should only take us about thirty minutes to get there, and we don't have to worry about getting lost."

"How long does it take if we walk?" I asked.

"I don't know. It's a big city. I have no problem walking. But you—"

"Don't worry about me. We'll walk." I had to be careful with my money in case we encountered problems.

We had the steamed buns we brought with us for supper and for breakfast the next morning, then set off.

The snow had stopped falling; a few inches covered the ground. Our feet sunk soundlessly into the soft surface. With each step, the snow seeped through and was transformed into sharp needles, biting my feet to numbness. The cold air was damp here. The wind stabbed at our bones as if our winter jackets were made of thin paper. In Henan, the winter was cold too, but it was dry, easier to endure.

More than an hour later, near a huge square, we finally saw a two-storey grey building. A big sign hung over the main entrance.

Snowflake read aloud, "Sichuan Provincial Government."

My fingers were stiff, and my feet felt like ice blocks. Snowflake's nose had turned red. Two guards with rifles stood by the entrance, one on each side. They wore thick green winter caps, overcoats, gloves and long boots that were dry. One looked to be in his twenties, the other in his thirties.

Snowflake approached the younger guard. "Comrade, we'd like to see Vice-Minister Chang Cheng."

"Who are you?"

Thank God he spoke Mandarin.

Snowflake said, "My husband is an old friend of Vice-Minister Chang Cheng. This is my mother-in-law. We have an urgent matter and must see the vice-minister."

The older guard marched over. "I can tell you are not from here. Where are you from, and what is your business?"

"We are from Henan," I said.

He took a step closer. "Henan, eh? And what's your business?"

Snowflake and I glanced at each other. We couldn't discuss our problem here on the street.

"We must discuss our business with the vice-minister," I said.

"The minister is very busy," the older guard said. I noticed he had dropped the word *vice*. "No one is allowed to see him without telling us what it is about."

"It's about . . ." My voice was weak and uncertain. How could I tell these strangers that my son was jailed and might die?

Snowflake spoke up, "Comrade, you must let us see Minister Chang Cheng. It's a matter of life or death. We will remember your kindness forever."

The younger guard showed interest. "Who is going to die, and why?"

"My son," I blurted out.

He stared at me and frowned. I had no choice but to take out the letter from my inside pocket. "It's all here. My son used to work with Minister Chang Cheng. He wrote a letter to him."

The older guard stretched out his hand, palm up.

"We need to hand-deliver it to Comrade Chang Cheng," I said, and stepped back.

"Either you give it to me, and I'll pass it to him, or you

go home with your letter. A minister can't just see anyone from the street."

Of course. He was a big shot now, and we were no-bodies. The distance between us was like between Heaven and Earth.

"It's our best shot." Snowflake tugged my sleeve.

So this was it. I was like a person who couldn't swim but had to plunge into deep water. "Fine," I said. "But we'll wait here for the answer."

"Minister Chang Cheng is not in his office today. Come back tomorrow at the same time."

Should I believe him? "Will you be here tomorrow?" I asked.

"Yes."

I handed him my son's life and pleaded, "Thank you, Comrade. Please make sure you hand-deliver this to Minister Chang Cheng."

"I will." He put the letter in his pocket.

Now my son's life was in a stranger's pocket. Had I made a mistake? It was like twelve years ago when Xiao and I tried to make the right decision: stay in Luoyang or go home. We went home and survived, but paid a terrible price. But this time, with one wrong move, Wu may die, and I would never be able to live with myself.

"Let's hire a rickshaw. I don't want you to catch a cold," Snowflake said.

I said nothing.

"Don't worry about money." Snowflake patted my hand gently. "I have brought some money. Let's hire a rickshaw."

I agreed.

We returned to our hotel room. Northwest winds shook

the window. The room felt like an ice cave. We huddled together under the quilt, trying to gain warmth from each other.

In the morning, more snow lay on the ground. Snowflake again insisted we take a rickshaw. We arrived at the provincial government building at the same time as the day before. I was relieved when I saw the same two guards.

"Comrade." I approached the older guard, feeling like a convicted criminal waiting for my sentence.

"I have the reply for you." He handed me the same envelope that I had given him the day before. I passed it to Snowflake. Her hands shook slightly when she opened the envelope. As she scanned the letter, her face turned white and she dropped to the ground like a sack of rice. The letter fell in the snow. I rushed to it before it was blown away. I flattened the piece of paper. It was Wu's letter alright, but a line in red ink was written at the bottom. I scrambled to the older guard, knelt at his feet and presented the letter as if I were making an offering to God.

"What does it say?"

He took the letter and read it aloud. "I have no recollection of this person whatsoever."

"It must be a mistake! Have you hand-delivered it to the minister?" I asked.

"Yes, I did."

"It's impossible. He knew my son. They worked together. Where is Chang Cheng's signature? Show me his signature." I was illiterate but not stupid. I knew what a signature looked like.

The guard sighed. "We don't use signatures. We use stamps."

"Then show me his stamp. Where is his stamp?" I clutched his overcoat and wouldn't let it go.

The younger guard came over. "If you dare to disturb the peace in front of a government building, you will be arrested."

A crowd had gathered by now. Snowflake lay in the snow with her eyes shut. Some onlookers tried to revive her.

"Please," I cried out, "I must see the minister!"

The older guard pried my hands off his coat and ran inside. A moment later, he came back with a bowl of hot water. He said something to the younger guard, then went to Snowflake and fed her the water. I crawled over to my daughter-in-law. She moaned and slowly opened her eyes, staring at the sky.

The younger guard hailed a rickshaw and squatted beside me. "Auntie, where are you staying? We can send you to the hotel. The fare is on us."

"I'm not leaving! I must see the minister," I dug my heels in, wouldn't budge.

Two more guards ran out, rifles in hand. What would they do? Kill us? Let them. I hadn't been killed by the Japanese, by Qi, by poverty or by famine. Now let them open fire on me—a member of the Underground Communists' Network and the mother of two Communist soldiers.

Chapter 29

The older guard inched his face to my ear. I could feel his hot breath. He whispered, "I strongly suggest you leave and never come back. If you refuse, you and this young lady will be arrested and charged as counter-revolutionaries for trying to rescue a traitor. If I were you, I would leave before it's too late. Now, tell me the name of the hotel."

Snowflake groaned. All blood drained from her face. I blinked. She was the mother of my grandchildren. She must be there for them.

I told the guard the hotel name.

I don't remember how we got in the rickshaw. When we arrived at the hotel, Red Nose helped get Snowflake inside. We put her in bed. Her forehead was as hot as burning coal. Red Nose brought us hot water. When I tried to feed Snowflake, she shook her head.

"Let me die. Let me die before Wu. I can't take it anymore." Tears rolled down her face like pearls from a broken string.

"Don't be silly," I said. "As long as the green hills are preserved, there will be no worry of firewood. You must be alive for Wu, for the children."

The next morning, Snowflake refused to eat. Her eyes had lost their shining gleam and were sunk deep in their sockets. Her hair was sticky from sweat.

Red Nose came in. "She needs a doctor," he said. I agreed but didn't have money for it. I had to leave enough for our train fare back.

"We need a stove," I said. "It's too cold here."

He shook his head and left the room.

I sat down heavily on the edge of the bed. With an effort, Snowflake lifted her head. "Help me unbutton my jacket."

"Why?" In such a cold room, we slept with our clothes on.

"I have some money in the inner pocket. I don't think we can leave tomorrow. We need money for the hotel."

I unbuttoned her jacket and found a few bills, just enough for another few days' hotel fees.

"I'll fetch a doctor for you," I said.

She said nothing but stuck out both hands from under the cover, showing me the pair of jade bracelets that I noticed when I first met her. She had never taken them off.

"These are the engagement gifts from Wu. Take them off and pawn them. It should be enough for a doctor and some medicine." My daughter-in-law's voice was as weak as a mosquito's buzz.

The bracelets slipped easily off her bony wrists. As I took them, my hands shook, as if I was stealing them from her. The pale green jade was silky and warm. Chinese believe that the longer a piece of jade jewelry is worn, the more its owner's flesh will enrich the jade's texture and mystical power and make it a talisman for its owner.

Maybe they were a talisman for her. Maybe they would save her life.

I will compensate you one day for all the suffering you've endured for our sake. I said in silence.

I asked Red Nose to take me to a pawn shop. The man's face brightened. He must have been worrying about our hotel fees. He also reminded me that now all the pawn shops were called consignment shops.

I pawned the bracelets for eighty yuan.

Red Nose fetched a doctor for Snowflake. He diagnosed Snowflake as having a very bad cold, plus extreme worry and anxiety made her condition worse. The doctor assured us that by taking his medicine, she would recover.

I was at Snowflake's bedside day and night, feeding her food, water and medicine. In the eight days until Snowflake was fit to travel again I forced myself not to think about whether Wu had been sentenced.

We arrived home on the ninth day. Orchid, Xiao and Snowflake's parents had been worried to death and were discussing whether Orchid should come to Chengdu to look for us. We all gathered at Master Chen's home, recounting what had happened.

"Why wouldn't he tell the truth?" Master Chen asked.

"I don't know," I said.

"Are you sure it was Chang Cheng's handwriting?" Orchid asked.

"At first, I didn't believe it. But when they paid for our rickshaw fare and threatened to arrest us if we wouldn't leave, I was sure they got the order from Chang Cheng," I said.

"But why? Wu had risked his own life to ensure Chang Cheng's safety!" Xiao growled.

"Maybe he doesn't want anyone to know he was a coward. With Wu out of the way, nobody will ever find out," Master Chen said.

"But Wu wouldn't tell anyone," I said.

"He told you," Orchid countered. "And now we all know it. There's no such wall that wind can't blow through. Chang Cheng is a high-ranking government official now. He can't afford to let the truth leak out."

Snowflake was quiet all this time. Suddenly, she screamed, "I want my husband back! I want my husband back!" She flailed about madly and swept the teacups off the table. Star and Moon clung to their mother and howled too. A female wolf with two cubs.

"Stop," Master Chen hushed his daughter. "You don't want the neighbours to hear."

"I don't care. I'll kill them all!"

Master Chen's eyes almost popped out of their sockets. He covered his daughter's mouth with his hand. "Are you crazy? Do you want to be arrested as well?"

Snowflake refused to eat and wash. Her parents had to force-feed her. She slept all day and cried all night; in a short time, her eyes were sunken and her face ashy. On top of all this, Orchid told me that she had tuberculosis and had to return home. She invited Xiao and I to move to Shaanxi so she could look after us.

But leaving meant giving up my house and the treasures buried in it. It also meant Qi could sleep better without us being around. I couldn't go.

"Ma, what makes you think you can get our house back?

Do you know how many landlords were killed during the land reform campaign? Keeping land deeds is a big crime now. You must let go," Orchid reasoned with me.

"But what about the treasure?" I asked.

"You have to let it go as well."

"How about Qi then? After he has done so many horrible things to our family, to other Chinese people, he is allowed to walk away?" I argued.

"Ma, this is an unjust world. You must realize this. Now the most important thing is to be alive. Besides, you and Xiao can hardly survive on your own. Let me help. I just need to go home to make some arrangements. Once I'm ready, I'll write to you," Orchid said resolutely.

Both Master Chen and Xiao agreed with Orchid. I finally said yes.

On the day of the public sentencing rally, I went with Xiao. By this time, Snowflake was half-mad and delirious. We felt that she couldn't withstand any more blows, so we didn't tell her about the rally.

On the stage, thirty-two "criminals" stood in rows, bent over and tied up by ropes in a *wu hua da bang* style—neck, chest, arms, hands and wrists bound by one thick rope forming a five-petal flower pattern. Behind each "criminal" stood two armed soldiers. I couldn't see my son's face. A placard stuck out behind their necks. After a wave of slogan shouting, the mayor of Kaifeng stepped onto the stage, cleared his throat and began to read out the sentences. I craned my neck, not daring to miss a single word. After thirty death penalties with immediate execution in a row, I was certain all those on stage would be dead today and could hardly keep myself sitting straight. Then I heard Wu's name and the fateful words, "Traitor and counter-revolutionary Li Wu is sentenced to death . . ."

I passed out.

When I woke up in the shed, it took me a moment to recognize the faces surrounding me: Xiao, Orchid, Master Chen and Mrs. Chen. I wailed, "My son is dead!"

"What are you talking about?" Orchid frowned.

"They sentenced Wu to death," I cried out.

"True, but with a two-year reprieve. You passed out before hearing the whole thing," Xiao said.

"So Wu is alive?" I was mad with happiness.

"Yes, yes." Master Chen and Mrs. Chen nodded eagerly.

"But he will be dead in two years, right?" Fresh tears welled up.

Master Chen said, "Consider Wu lucky because only two out of thirty-two showcased today are still alive. They will be shipped to Xinjiang to serve their sentences. You never know, sometimes prisoners with good behaviour get sentences reduced. As long as the green hills are preserved, there will be no worry of firewood."

I promised my husband to keep the house and family together. Not only had I lost our house, but I had also lost a son and would never be able to see him again. But I felt like an ant being thrown into an ocean, unable to fight the enormous waves. Nobody could.

Chapter 30

Three weeks later, Orchid's letter arrived. With the money she sent me, we bought train tickets and headed to the village of Maixiang, meaning "wheat land," where Orchid and her husband lived in Shaanxi province. They settled us into a small rented courtyard near campus housing. My son-in-law was a very nice man. He helped Orchid provide for us. Xiao soon found a job in the college's canteen as a cook and our life seemed to return to normal.

Orchid warned us never to tell anyone about Wu. With his impending death hanging above my head like a sword, I could only cry soundlessly in the middle of the night. What this world had become where a mother couldn't grieve openly for her son! My heart also ached for Zhong, who I had not seen since our parting in Luoyang fourteen years ago and probably wouldn't again. Orchid had told me some horrible stories about his wife. I was sure she was the one who kept him away.

A year after Xiao and I moved to Maixiang, Daisy showed up unexpectedly with two children and the horrible news of Big Ox's death.

When the Suppression of Counter-Revolutionaries

Campaign began, Chairman Mao said 95% of people were good; but 5% were true counter-revolutionaries. The head of Big Ox's village had not been able to fill his 5% counter-revolutionaries quota. So he went to the nice man, Big Ox, asking him to put his name forward as a counter-revolutionary. That idiot agreed as easily as we would agree to do a small favour for a neighbour. Six months passed—nothing happened. Then an order came from above. All declared counter-revolutionaries were to be arrested and shot. Big Ox's death left Daisy with a two-year-old girl, Hui, and a seven-month-old boy, Ming.

"You know what they did after they killed my husband? They sent me a bill for forty-five cents for the cost of the bullet!" Daisy wailed.

Now that our family had grown to five, Orchid moved us into a bigger courtyard. Then we heard excellent news from Wu. Due to good behaviour, his death sentence had been commuted to life in prison. A big stone in my heart was lifted, and I could breathe again. As long as Wu was alive, we had hope. Orchid came to my place, and we held a secret celebration. We also learned that upon receiving this news, Snowflake was returning to her normal self. Master Chen had lost his restaurant to the government during the Transformation of Private Enterprises to State-Owned Entities Campaign. Now the previous owner worked as a cook in the same restaurant, and Snowflake and her mother stayed at home, looking after the kids.

When Wen showed up on my doorstep, it was the happiest moment for me in a long time. I hadn't seen him since he left home at age sixteen. Now he was a thirty-two-year-old army surgeon. He stayed with us for a week and convinced Daisy to go to northeast China, where he worked, to get the lump in her lower back surgically removed. Daisy left Hui and Ming in my care. After the surgery, Daisy found a job as a primary school teacher in the military factory where Wen worked, hoping to make some money so she could afford to bring Hui and Ming to live with her. However, the authorities found out about her counter-revolutionary husband, and the school fired her. Furthermore, they planned to ship her back to Big Ox's village in Hubei. Going back meant becoming a peasant again and being watched closely by the villagers. With her health condition, she could die. Wen had to make a decision fast. He found a factory worker to marry Daisy so she could remain in the factory as a housewife. This way at least she would keep her urban residential status. As a newlywed without an income of her own, she couldn't take Hui and Ming back for the time being.

Our life in the village was not worry-free either. The head of the Street Committee—once a shoemaker—had been harassing Orchid, Xiao and me from day one. He tried to pry into our past with a determination that nine cows couldn't pull back. Orchid finally found a cooking job for Xiao in Xi'an City, a two-and-a-half-hour train ride away. Xiao and I moved there with Hui and Ming. We were temporarily assigned to two rooms in Northwestern University's guest house, right next to a public washroom. Water seeped through the cracks in the wall, and the rooms were very damp all year round. But "temporary" became two years, and the cold, wet air triggered pain in my joints. I developed rheumatoid arthritis and became paralyzed and bedridden. If not for Xiao, I wouldn't have survived.

Life had played out in the most unexpected way. My husband, a successful tile flipper, didn't even own a hole in the ground, and I, a house filler, didn't have a house to fill.

≈

Road's End

XI'AN CITY,
SHAANXI PROVINCE

1966

≈

Chapter 31

I know my days are numbered. When longevity is living to age seventy, reaching age seventy-four is a surprise.

In our rented apartment in this four-storey residential building, the heat is stifling in July. Outside is a tree-lined boulevard. Earlier in the year, the Great Proletarian Cultural Revolution began, attracting many young people. They often parade along the boulevard, passing by our building. The beating of gongs and drums and the shouting are so noisy that I can't have a minute of peace. I feel the damp shirt on my body. A pallet in the middle of the bed covers the chamber pot beneath it. Xiao made this special bed for me. He has been my caretaker for the last eight years: bathing me, washing my mangled feet and regularly dumping the contents from my chamber pot, keeping the room odour-free. Xiao does it all, except wrapping my feet for me every day. I no longer can walk, so there's no need to bind them.

How the world has changed. For thousands of years in China, women with bound feet were desirable. To marry well, we complied with the cruel tradition. Our bare, distorted feet were considered erotic. Not even a hundred years have passed. Women with bound feet are now like dinosaurs, like historical ruins. We still won't show our feet, more because of shame than secrecy, but I no longer care. Both Hui and Ming have seen them. However, relying on somebody else to wash them for me is embarrassing, even when that person is Xiao.

Twenty-nine years ago, when Xiao came to Kaifeng looking for me, he was seventeen, and I was forty-four. We have only been separated for ten days when I went to Chengdu with Snowflake to save Wu's life. If there's any unfinished business for me, anyone I feel deeply indebted to and guilty about, it is Xiao. We stopped having sex many years ago, but he refused to take on a wife. I'm glad I persuaded him to adopt Ming. At least now Xiao has a son to take care of him in his old age, bury him when the time comes and burn joss sticks and paper money for him during the tomb-sweeping days of *Qingming*. This is vitally important to all Chinese.

"Do you want some water?" Xiao asks.

"Yes."

Both Hui and Ming have joined the revolution and dart in and out of the flat like bees. They are not at home right now. To get the entire family to come to say the final goodbye is every dying person's last wish, and yet for me, it won't happen.

My eldest son, Zhong, is far away, in Guangdong province, southeast China. He is an accountant working for a state-owned farm for the Chinese that returned from overseas after the liberation. Zhong is lucky; he hasn't ended up in jail because he quit the Nationalist Army before the civil war. He and his wife went to Guangdong right after the liberation because in her hometown, her entire clan is there to help them. With Zhong's English skills and accountant experience, he is a perfect fit for working with those once-overseas Chinese. The last time I saw him was on the day he joined the Nationalist Army in Luoyang, twenty-eight years ago. Even though Zhong writes to me from time to time and sends family photos, it's not enough to fill the hole in my heart.

At least I have seen Wen a couple of times since he left home. I turn to look at the two framed photos on the desk, one of Wen with his wife and two children, the other of Daisy with her new husband. Hui and Ming visited their mother a couple of times when they were old enough but they hardly remember their biological father. Perhaps it's a good thing. This way they don't suffer much. Big Ox was in no way a counter-revolutionary. He was just a silly man, so silly that he got himself shot. When I see him on the other side, I'll have to give him a good scolding for leaving his family in that horrible condition.

My deepest pain, my biggest failure as a mother, is Wu. The last time I had a glimpse of him was at that public rally in Kaifeng. Ocean waves of heads and pumping fists were between me and the stage where he stood with the other accused criminals. Heads bowed low, they were all tied up in a five-petal flower pattern. I now know Xinjiang is a remote, harsh northwest territory thousands of li away. The prison is in the middle of a desert. People say even without prison walls, nobody can escape. Those who tried either died of thirst and starvation or froze to death, their corpses turning into dried-up mummies. I don't even have a recent photo of him. Because visitation is not allowed, the image of him in my mind remains the same as when he was twenty-nine.

My youngest daughter, Orchid, and her husband, Tong Shu, are the nearest to me—only a three-hour train ride away. How I wish to see her one last time, to have one of my children at my deathbed. I guess it's hard to time a person's death, and Tong Shu can't just leave his job at the university anytime he wants.

Yaoyao, my youngest granddaughter, is only four, a cute little girl with curious eyes and two little dimples when she smiles. The only time we met, when I touched her soft, curly hair, love swelled in my heart. I told her I had stories to tell her when she grew up. I have tried to tell Ming our family stories, but he seems not so interested. We Chinese believe the more sons, the more blessings, but it's not always true. Yaoyao, at age two, on the other hand, not only planned her escape from the daycare centre, but also took her belongings with her. If Orchid hadn't sworn it's true, I may not have believed it. If any of my grandchildren will pass our family history to the next generation, it will be Yaoyao. But my time is running out. I can only whisper the stories in her dreams when I cross over to the other side.

I have waited so long to get my family back but with a *ten thousand unwillingness*, I have to let that wish go.

I don't know how to face my late husband if he's waiting for me on the other side. I have lost our property, along with Wen's treasure buried in it, and I have failed to keep my family together.

I'm longing for the sun to set so we can open the windows and let the cool breeze drift in. But I don't know if I can hang on that long.

"Golden Dove, how are you feeling?" Xiao calls me by

my name from our previous life. When Hui and Ming are not around, there's no need to pretend.

I open my eyes, reach for his hand and whisper, "For what I owe you, I'll repay you in our next life." With all my might, I give his hand a final squeeze, and let go.

Epilogue

During Golden Phoenix's final days, Xiao took one month off from work to care for her. However, upon returning to work after her burial, Xiao discovered that he wouldn't receive a pay cheque for that month. He argued with his supervisor, pointing out that when he asked for the leave permit, no one said anything about time off without pay. Besides, others got paid when they took time off. The supervisor said it was his fault for not asking the question. In addition, other people took time off either for themselves or for their immediate family members. Xiao was only looking after an aunt. "Where were her own children?" the supervisor asked. Xiao had nothing to say about that. Even though Golden Phoenix was indeed his wife, he felt like a mute person consuming bitter herbs, unable to express his grievances.

On Xiao's way home, his emotions churned, a tumultuous mix of pent-up anger, a sense of being wronged, and grief from Golden Phoenix's death—a blazing fireball in his chest. It was the peak of summer, intensifying the heat within him, so he bought ten popsicles to cool himself down. Little did he know that consuming a large amount of cold food during extremely hot weather could, according to Chinese medicine, potentially lead to stomach and intestinal spasms, or diarrhea.

That night, he was doubled over by excruciating stomach cramps. Beads of sweat as large as soybeans streamed down his face as he twisted and turned all night. By the next morning, pale as a ghost, he was unable to sit up. Hui and Ming hastily borrowed a flatbed cart and rushed him to the Number One People's Hospital. To their dismay, the doctor informed them that Xiao likely suffered from *jiao chang sha*, a severe intestinal condition that required surgery. But not one surgeon was available—they had all been suspended from work to be criticized, denounced, and reformed by the revolutionary masses.

In their desperation, Hui and Ming eventually sent a telegram to their mother in northeast China. Upon receiving the distressing news, their Uncle Wen swiftly tapped into his network of contacts and managed to secure a permit from the Shaanxi provincial government, granting him permission to perform surgery on Xiao.

Wen embarked on a gruelling journey, travelling day and night by train to Xi'an, but it was still too late. Xiao had passed away three hours earlier. The poor man was in so much pain that he chewed his bedsheet and his mouth had to be pried open to remove the wad of fabric. Wen insisted on conducting an autopsy, which revealed that 90% of Xiao's intestines had putrefied. Wen believed that if Xiao had the surgery nine days ago, when he first fell ill, his life probably would have been saved.

Northwestern University's policy when an employee passed away was to take back his living quarters. Wen advocated for Ming, highlighting that he was still a minor and that the university, Xiao's employer, bore some responsibility for Xiao's untimely death. Also, weren't the working class, alongside peasants and soldiers, the masters of the new China? Ultimately, Hui and Ming were permitted to stay in the flat until they reached the age of majority. Orchid and Tong Shu assumed total financial responsibility for the children.

From the onset of the Cultural Revolution, various factions emerged within almost every working unit, with rebels and loyalists becoming fierce rivals. Hui became the leader of the loyalist faction in her school, which made her a target for the rebels. Faced with threats to her life, she fled to Guangxi province, where she sought protection in the home of one of Wen's former comrades. Ming, too, did not remain at home for long. In December of 1968, Chairman Mao called for educated youth to "go up to the mountains and down to the villages" to be re-educated by peasants. Alongside millions of Chinese "educated youth," Ming, barely out of junior high, answered Chairman Mao's call and was sent to rural Gansu to work as a peasant.

At this juncture, the household of Golden Phoenix had dissipated into the dust of history.

The Pinioned Bird
1938–1970

By now, the college administration had been replaced by two teams. One, the Revolutionary Committee, was formed from within the college. The factories in the nearby cities sent the other team, the Mao Zedong Thoughts Propaganda Team of the Working Class.

The Revolutionary Committee took my husband's case seriously. Just before the liberation[1], Tong Shu had received a list of students who were either underground Communists or Communist sympathizers from the Nationalist government. As the acting dean of the Nationalist-owned college, he was instructed to arrange for their arrests. But Tong Shu managed to warn those students; only after they all escaped did he hand the list to the police. A decade and a half later, however, during the Cultural Revolution, Tong Shu was accused of having the former students arrested and he was locked up. During the investigation, the Revolutionary Committee tracked down

---

[1] The Communist Party called winning the civil war "the liberation."

each blacklisted name and, finding all of them alive and well, some even holding important positions within the party and the government, thus cleared Tong Shu of this particular charge. Nonetheless, he was still labelled as a member of the *black class* and remained in the *cowshed* because he was guilty of being a professor and having old customs and ideas.

I was only too relieved that Yaoyao didn't witness her father being showcased on the stage during class struggle meetings; neither was she around for the horrible ordeal that her friend Lily's mother brought on me. My decision to send Yaoyao away to live with her sister in the Qin Mountains now seemed even more brilliant.

It began when that wicked woman came to borrow some paper from me, to write yet another self-criticizing essay. I dragged out a box of white paper from underneath the bed and gave some to her.

In the evening, two men wearing red arm bands visited me.

"Are you Tong Shu's family?" the dark one asked.

"Yes, I am." In the new society, words like husband and wife, even spouse, were abolished, replaced either by *airen*[2] or family.

"We're the representatives of the Propaganda Team of the Working Class."

"What's the matter?"

"We need you to come with us to answer a few questions about Tong Shu."

"Yes, of course." The Propaganda Team of the Working

---

[2] *airen*: literally meaning lover, it really refers to a legally married spouse.

Class held ultimate power over us, and there was no way to avoid them. I locked the door and went with the men. It was already dark outside, though there weren't many stars.

They headed to an academic building and led me into a small room. All the windows were covered by black cloth. I had to close my eyes for a moment against the bright light thrown out from the bare bulb hanging from the ceiling. Behind the desk sat a young woman and beside her stood a man.

"Li Xiulan, do you know why you are here?" the woman asked.

"I don't."

"We need you to expose your airen, Tong Shu, for any wrongdoing."

"He has confessed everything: his family background, his desire to become an expert in his field—"

"More! There's more!" She shot up and came around from behind the desk. Her big-toed working boots struck the ground: *thump, thump.*

"What more?" I was confused.

"You know what I'm talking about. This is your last chance to turn him in, to defend the Great Proletariat Cultural Revolution."

I was puzzled. "I have already told the Revolutionary Committee everything about Tong Shu."

"Liar!" the twenty-something female tiger roared, her face inches away from mine. I didn't expect a young woman could be so vicious.

"Tong Shu is an American spy. Confess!"

An American spy? Where was that coming from? "I

know everything about Tong Shu. He might have been a bourgeoisie but not a spy."

"Make her talk!" she barked to the three men.

One man, young and strong, held my neck from behind with a powerful grip, twisted me around and released me. I was like a top spinning around before collapsing into a lotus pose on the floor with my legs neatly folded on the ground. I tried to push myself up but the woman stomped on my hands with her heavy boots. I screamed and crumpled back to the floor. They took turns kicking me and yelling at me, demanding I get up. When I finally managed to stand, the man twisted my neck again and the process repeated. I had never known such a torture technique, almost a form of art.

After what seemed an eternity, I was half-dead. The torturers were also exhausted.

"So you are the type who won't cry without seeing the coffin," the woman sounded resigned. "Show her the evidence."

A man took out a sheet of paper from a desk drawer and shoved it into my face. I stared at the blank page.

"What's this?" My voice was so weak I could hardly hear it myself.

He held it up against the light. I finally saw it—a row of faint English letters appeared on the paper.

"What does this mean?" I asked.

"That's what we want to find out. That's why you are here," the woman shouted.

"If I understood these letters, I wouldn't ask you. How does it have anything to do with us?"

"Your friend tipped us off, the friend you lent the paper

to. These must be the secret codes used by spies—spies like Tong Shu."

The fog cleared. This was from the stack of paper I had given to Lily's mother. She was the one who had reported me.

I gathered all my strength and said, "As far as I know, Tong Shu bought the paper in Beijing at a yard sale from American soldiers when the war ended. I don't know anything about those English words."

After that, I passed out.

When I opened my eyes again, a fifty-ish man's face loomed above me. Through the now uncovered windows, the sky appeared violet-blue.

"I'm very sorry for what happened." The man helped me up to sit on a stool. "I'm Zhou Zhicheng, the team leader. You can call me Zhou Shifu. No one reported the interrogation to me; they certainly shouldn't have used extreme measures. It was a terrible mistake," he apologized profusely. Zhou Shifu looked like an old factory worker, a kind one.

"Just tell me what's going on." My voice was hoarse.

"Have some water first." He poured water from a thermos bottle into an old white enamel mug and handed it to me.

"When my team didn't get the confession from you, they reported to me. I sent a member on the first train to Xi'an this morning with the evidence. The police there had the English characters examined. It turns out they are watermarks. After they called me and told me the result, I rushed here. I'm so very sorry."

What could I say? Demanding an apology was out of the question. So many were locked up or beaten without any evidence. Some even committed suicide. I was lucky that I was still alive.

The team leader accompanied me all the way home. I had difficulty walking and had to hold onto his arm.

I couldn't sit or lie down for a week because my back and buttocks hurt so much, neither could I lie on my stomach due to my badly bruised ribs. So I knelt on the bed with a pile of soft pillows under my belly. I vowed never to talk to Lily's mother again and to forbid Yaoyao from playing with her friend ever again. I was sure that witch had done this to save her husband and get him released. Perhaps she thought she had caught a real spy, but her plan failed because of the false report. After all the things I had done for her, this was how she repaid me. What a black-hearted woman!

MAJOR CHINESE HISTORICAL
EVENTS 1912–1966

1912: China experienced the Xinhai Revolution, resulting in the overthrow of the Qing Dynasty after more than 260 years of imperial rule. This led to the establishment of the Republic of China on January 1, 1912, with Sun Yat-sen (also known as Sun Zhongshan) becoming its first provisional president.

1921: Founding of the Communist Party of China (CPC). On July 1, 1921, the Communist Party of China was founded in Shanghai. The party emerged from a meeting of various Marxist groups and intellectuals seeking to establish a revolutionary movement in China.

1927: First United Front and the Northern Expedition. In 1927, the Chinese Nationalist Party (Kuomintang or KMT) under the leadership of Chiang Kai-shek (also known as Jiang Jieshi) formed an alliance with the Communist Party of China known as the First United Front. The United Front aimed to unify China and rid the country of warlords. They launched the Northern Expedition, a military campaign to defeat the warlords and unite the country under KMT rule. However, tensions between the two factions grew due to ideological differences and disagreements over leadership and strategies. The alliance between the KMT and the CPC began to unravel, leading to a split and eventually the start of a violent conflict between the two parties.

1931: Mukden Incident. On September 18, the Japanese military, using an explosion on the South Manchurian Railway as a pretext, launched an attack near Mukden (now Shenyang) in northeastern China. This event marked the beginning of the Japanese invasion and occupation of Manchuria, leading to the establishment of the puppet state of Manchukuo.

1936: The Xi'an Incident took place in December 1936 when General Zhang Xueliang, a Chinese warlord, kidnapped Chiang Kai-shek, the leader of the Nationalist Party. This incident led to a temporary truce between the Nationalists and Communists and the formation of the Second United Front against Japan.

1937: Marco Polo Bridge Incident. On July 7, 1937, hostilities erupted near the Marco Polo Bridge (also known as the Lugou Bridge) outside Beiping (now called Beijing). This incident marked the beginning of the full-scale conflict between China and Japan, known as the Second Sino-Japanese War. Following the fall of Nanjing (also known as Nanking) to Japanese forces in December 1937, the city experienced a horrific atrocity known as the

Nanjing Massacre. Japanese soldiers subjected the city's residents to widespread rape, murder and other forms of brutal violence, resulting in the deaths of hundreds of thousands of Chinese civilians and disarmed soldiers.

1938: Japanese military force occupied Kaifeng and many other cities and areas in Henan province. The occupation brought significant hardships and suffering to the local population. The occupation of Kaifeng resulted in the destruction of infrastructure, cultural sites and historical landmarks. The population suffered from scarcity of food and resources.

1945: In August, Japan officially surrendered to the Allies, effectively ending World War II. This victory had a major impact on China, as it marked the end of the Japanese occupation and brought an end to years of conflict and suffering. While World War II had ended, the Chinese Civil War between the Nationalist Party (Kuomintang) led by Chiang Kai-shek and the Communist Party of China led by Mao Zedong resumed.

1949: On October 1, 1949, the Communist Party of China, led by Mao Zedong, officially proclaimed the establishment of the People's Republic of China (PRC). This marked the culmination of the Chinese Communist Party's victory in the long-running Chinese Civil War against the Nationalist Party (Kuomintang or KMT). With the establishment of the PRC, the Communist Party gained control over mainland China, while the KMT retreated to the island of Taiwan.

1966: The Great Proletarian Cultural Revolution, commonly referred to as the Cultural Revolution, began in China. The socio-political movement led by Chairman Mao Zedong involved the mobilization of the Red Guards, primarily composed of students, who rebelled against traditional values and targeted intellectuals deemed counter-revolutionary. This period witnessed mass mobilization, public denunciations and the persecution of intellectuals. Historical sites and cultural artifacts were destroyed, and political power struggles within the Communist Party intensified. The Cultural Revolution caused widespread social disruption, economic setbacks, and lasting divisions within Chinese society. It gradually came to an end after Mao's death in 1976, leaving a profound and lasting impact on China's history and culture.

ACKNOWLEDGEMENTS

As an immigrant to Canada with English being my second language and battling a long-term disability, it took me almost 20 years to complete the China China trilogy. *The House Filler* is the first book of the trilogy, and I am immensely grateful that it has finally come to fruition. I often liken my journey to climbing Mount Everest in a wheelchair. Without those who pushed and pulled me along the way, reaching this summit would have been impossible.

I am deeply grateful for the assistance provided by the following individuals: Rick Borger, Madelaine Shaw-Wong, and Chris Kemp-Jackson, for their thoughtful critique, painstaking effort, and lasting friendship; Theanna Bischoff, Michelle Browne, and Elizabeth Stock for their freelance editing and Professor David Wright, for his assistance in translating Chinese lyrics and ancient Chinese poems into English in the trilogy. Furthermore, I would like to extend my heartfelt appreciation to the Alexandra Writers' Centre Society and the Writers' Guild of Alberta. The support and opportunities provided through their 2019 Borderlines Writers Circle Calgary program led me to meet my mentor, Sandra McIntyre. Her advice and guidance were invaluable. I also had the great fortune of participating in the 2021 Emerging Writers Incentive program, offered by the esteemed Banff Centre for the Arts and Creativity. This long journey reached its biggest milestone when I met Wendy Atkinson at Ronsdale Press and their editor, Robyn So. I owe Wendy the gratitude for believing in me, and Robyn for making my final draft shine.

My next acknowledgement is rather unusual. As we all know, it has become increasingly rare for publishers and literary agents to respond to queries, which unfortunately has become an industry norm. However, back in 2013, I submitted a novella with eight chapters to NeWest Press. In General Manager Paul Matwychuk's rejection letter, he not only provided the reasons behind the rejection but also suggested that I expand the novella, as he sensed there was a larger story waiting to be told. Ten years later, I have expanded the original novella into a trilogy. I have also kept that rejection letter to this day as a reminder of the difference Mr. Matwychuk made in my life.

Last, but certainly not least, I want to express my heartfelt gratitude to my best friend, Dusan Milutinovic, for being my most enthusiastic cheerleader, my walking dictionary and my unpaid editor, and for his unwavering belief in me, even during times when I doubted myself.

ABOUT THE AUTHOR

Tong Ge, born and raised in China, arrived in Canada in the late 80s as an international student. She began writing the China China trilogy in 2004 with the first book: *The House Filler*. Although she was challenged by learning to write in English and by her long-term disability, she persevered and since 2012 has published poetry and prose in English and Chinese in publications such as *Prism*, *Ricepaper*, *Flow*, *Canadian Stories*, and *The Polyglot*. In addition, she has won three literary awards and has been short- and long-listed for another five. Tong Ge lives in Calgary, Alberta.